The (Mis)adventures Of a Dumbarton Maths Teacher

Bappi Bhattacharyya

Copyright © 2024 Bappi Bhattacharyya
All rights reserved.
ISBN: 9798877993938

DEDICATION

I'd like to thank a lady whose name I don't know but who I last spoke to in 1989 when she phoned me on behalf of Strathclyde Regional Council. I believe I was out when she first called but she kindly phoned again instead of just going to the next name on the list.

Whoever you are, I am eternally grateful to you.

CONTENTS

1 The New Arrival
2 The First Morning
3 The Times They Are A-Changin'
4 The Staffroom
5 First Class
6 The Morning Interval
7 The Rest of the Department
8 In the Beginning
9 It's Quite an Easy Job (Really?)
10 The Headie
11 Comic Relief and Che Guevara - Eat yer Heart Out
12 Johnny Goldenballs
13 Room Thirteen
14 Useful In-service
15 A Christmas Tale
16 Silvermints, Tayto Crisps and Why You Don't Mess with the Irish
17 Spain – Thank God There Were No Selfies Back Then!
18 Spain – The Invasion
19 Spain – Sailing if You're a Kid Capsizing if You're Not
20 Alton Towers – Where Nothing Ever Goes Wrong
21 It Goes Horribly Wrong at Alton Towers
22 Rant Mode – It Doesn't Really Have to

	Make Sense
23	AIF(Hell)
24	Sperm Counts
25	The Saga of Professor Bon Jovi
26	When All You Really Need is a Motorbike
27	Driven Up the Walls With OCD
28	Smoking in the Classroom - It's Political Correctness Gone Mad
29	The Origin of the Word 'Dozen'
30	Pupil Voice
31	Dress for Success
32	Name and Number
33	Students – The Good, The Bad and The Pratts
34	Sex and Comic Book Characters
35	Drugs – They Really Are Bad for Your Arse
36	(Not) Working Through Your Lunch Hour
37	Night Buses
38	Classroom (Im)posters – They Need Hanged So They Do
39	School Dances
40	The (Day After) The St Patrick's Day Massacre
41	Classroom Visits and Why You Should Always Read Your Emails
42	What Happens to the Pupils who Can't do 'Anything?'
43	Parents Evenings
44	It's A Long Way to the Top
45	Simmered Peppers and Chinese Babies
46	Why Tracing Paper is So Expensive
47	Never Let a Kid Tell a Joke
48	Imelda
49	Activities Week – Johnston Style
50	The Other Departments
51	Smart Boards – The Naked Truth

52 Fire Prevention
53 Mary
54 The Crit
55 The Battle of Crosslet Road
56 Travelling With a Name Like Mine
57 The Journey Here
58 Grannied
59 Belt Up
60 PogWatch
61 Best Answer Ever
62 Spiriting Up Their Interest
63 The Bob Johnston Scale of Learning
64 Out of this Black and White World
65 Snow Fun Being a Professional
66 Change – For Better or for Worse

ACKNOWLEDGMENTS

I would like to thank my excellent friend and ex-colleague Peter Murray for going through this collection of my bizarre thoughts and ideas to start with to see if it was possible for it to be a goer or not. He said it is, so you can blame him. He also wrote the very kind foreword. I hope all my apostrophes are in the right places.

Go look up Whoops Apostrophe if you want to know why.

FOREWORD

"School, eh? We all have to go, and then get through it all! To return there again and TEACH is such a crazy choice?! "Those who can, do! Those who can't …teach! "is such an amusing proverb yet erroneous as (my good friend) Mr. Bhattacharyya shows us even if through his mercurial 'Carry on Teaching' type tales, told through his own eyes and experiences as a Maths' teacher at Dumbarton Academy – on four separate occasions!!!!!

The Good, the Bad, and the… well everything!

From the ancient to the new school, from teachers to pupils, to those vital Cleaners! And he tells it all with his tongue firmly in his cheek, for the craziness, the successes, and the truths…the Staffroom, the Inspectorate, In-Service, School Dances…
The anecdotes abound of course – his witty Chapter titles alone tell all, and the humour is non-stop. Lovely yet also mad pupils (and teachers!); Staff 5-a-side football to Academy School Trips – Alton Towers and abroad…
And all is told with a mischievous yet truthful glint in his eye! Bravo!"

Mr. Murray (English).

PROLOGUE

Location :   A maths classroom in Dumbarton Academy

Date :   Honestly could be one of many really, but likely sometime in the 90's

Time :   About 8-50am

The bell rang.

It was all downhill after that.

INTRODUCTION

Right, everybody, ok guys, everyone settle down and get ready please, come on.

Does that sound a little bit familiar to any of you?

For perhaps several thousand pupils this might take you back.

Ok, so if this works, then the stories I am going to tell will hopefully give you a few laughs and perhaps even, maybe a little sympathy for many members of the teaching profession.

If it doesn't, however, and merely gives credit to your despair and anguish at the state of education in this country these days then that's fine with me too.

So, let's make a start and to paraphrase the one and only Mick Jagger,

'Please allow me to introduce myself, I'm a man of wealth and taste.'

Well, to be honest, I'm not sure if either of these statements is completely (or remotely) true.

But overall I've not done too badly, and I have always stuck to my own particular taste and views in and about many things, so if you hang around long enough, and, given you've already shelled out a couple of quid for this mighty opus, I suspect you're probably quite likely to; then this will hopefully become a bit more clear as we travel together through the 80's, 90's 00's etc.

Ok. So, firstly, who am I?

My name is Bappi Bhattacharyya. I usually get referred to as Mr B, but quite often get my full and somewhat unofficial title, 'That Bastard Bhattacharyya.'
Notice that it's never 'That bastard B.' That has actually only just occurred to me as I wrote this. And coincidentally you will indeed hear a tale relating to this later on.

Well, one problem I have, is that given the only people probably reading this will already know me, this next part seems a bit superfluous but as they say 'them's the rules'.

First of all, the relevant bit that anyone perusing these tales needs to know, is that I have been for many years, (too many years in fact), a secondary school maths teacher and that a great deal of that time was spent in one school in particular. Dumbarton Academy.

I have also worked in a couple of other schools during my career, they get a bit of a mention too, and I also worked for several years in the pharmaceutical industry firstly, for Merck Pharmaceuticals and then Aventis Pharma (who actually headhunted me believe it or not!!) but most of my working career has been spent in secondary education.

I've quite an unusual teaching career in that I've left that school three times, so I am in quite a unique position to describe the issues and changes around the school and how it has developed over the years for better or worse, but to be honest that is not the main theme here and it only gets lightly touched on.

Now, a little bit about the town of Dumbarton. It's quite an interesting place. It is not particularly wealthy and not particularly poor. A bit of a mixture in fact.
As is the situation for many places, the people who live there in the vast majority are thoroughly decent people wanting the best for their children. On the whole the 'Sons of the Rock' as the natives get called are respectful, supportive and talented and over the years I did indeed have many great times. To be honest, I like the place and the people.

Ok, so why have I written this book?

Well, there's a couple of reasons.

Firstly: - The main reason is that it's just a way of me remembering a lot of good times with many of the best people I have ever met. (That's staff **and** pupils by the way.)

Over the years teaching has really changed and these stories, tales and anecdotes are actually all true. As you delve into this, it may seem to be a tad surprising, but they really genuinely are unless of course I get sued in which case it's all a fabrication of a warped mind or perhaps a Bobby Ewing coming out of the shower scenario type thing. It may also therefore be surmised that sometimes indeed the truth is a little bit stranger than fiction.

When I tell people about these events, they, more often than not, refuse to believe how things used to be, what really was not that long ago and what we got away with back in the day as we say. It is a real shame. I realise that much of this makes that time period seem very unprofessional, but I always point out when challenged about this, that despite all these shenanigans and chaotic situations, the results were much better in those days and the kids and staff were a helluva lot happier. Just putting it out there folks.

I was going to change the names of the people in the book (to protect the 'Guilty') but after a period of swithering I decided not to, as nothing bad at all is said about anyone. At least, at no time do I genuinely mean to insult or offend anyone at all. Basically, if your name gets mentioned it's probably because I like you. That's it. Even if I don't mention you, I probably still like you. I have though avoided mentioning any (virtually any) of the pupils' names as you never know how that would go down. I also don't put the boot in to anybody. You won't find out the three people (two pupils, one member of staff) that I hated.

Three out of more than ten thousand is probably not a bad ratio and certainly not worth bothering about.

Also, this is not a book about how unfair the job is, or the various stresses and injustices in the system, anyone could write that and I'm sure they already have. It's just a bit of a laugh and also, it's just to see if I could put together something that vaguely resembles a competent set of tales. If you are one of those teachers who convinces yourself that teachers really need these long holidays more than any other workers, the book's not for you either. You won't like it. Take it back. Ask for your money back!!

I hope any people from Dumbarton, on the off chance they get to see it, like it, and perhaps recognise themselves or colleagues in it whether you were a pupil or staff member, and if you are not from Dumbarton and somehow or other miraculously get to read the book then hopefully you just enjoy the tales. I have tried to paint a little picture of what life was like for a young teacher a couple of decades ago and how enjoyable an experience it generally was.

The stories are true, though obviously there's a little bit of creativity from time to time especially in terms of the conversations, and I've tried to reflect the sometimes 'choice' language that does get used. If that offends then I'm sorry. Maybe read it after 9pm.

It is also not in perfect chronological order as I can't remember the order all the events happened in, but it generally does follow a Then to Now direction.

Please accept my apologies for an extreme lack of writing talent.
Be gentle with me. It's my first (and last) time!
Dumbarton Academy, it definitely has to be said. You've made a happy man very old.

Secondly: - If enough people buy this bloody thing, I can *finally* chuck teaching!!!

This book is an attempt to acknowledge our gratitude, appreciation and absolute respect, on behalf of myself and Peter Murray for our 'school dad' who looked out for us and pretty much protected us from ourselves for years. We don't just like him, we love him and he's our absolute all-time hero - for Bob Johnston.

1 THE NEW ARRIVAL

I arrived at Dumbarton Academy (for the first time) on a bright sunny Monday morning in the August of 1989. I had received the call on the previous Friday afternoon from a lady working for Strathclyde Regional Council Education department telling me to go there.

My first impressions of the school were that it looked really ancient. I wasn't even sure if I was going through the correct entrance, but I just followed some staff through the car park and in through the somewhat overly large brown storm doors.

I think these things could have stopped a nuclear bomb blast. They were that big.

I knocked on the little office window on the right-hand side.

'Hi, I'm the maternity leave cover for maths,' I said. There was a very nice lady behind the window, who paused and then looked at me rather strangely.

I wondered what was wrong.

'Oh crap! Am I at the right place', I panicked, suddenly remembering there were, after all, other schools in Dumbarton.

To this day I hope and assume that I only said this in my head and didn't say what I was thinking out loud.

'I'll just go and get Mr. McDonald,' she said.

2 THE FIRST MORNING

My first interaction with a member of the teaching staff of this wonderful educational establishment was with Mr John McDonald who even then looked like the Mr Rumbold character from the old sitcom, 'Are You Being Served?' He was, at the time, what they called an Assistant Head Teacher.
The conversation went something along these lines.

He first asked me if I had a contract yet and I told him, as I had told the nice office lady, that I was only 'covering a maternity leave.'

When he burst out laughing, I started to get quite worried. After seeing my startled look, he kindly started to explain.
"That maternity leave is for Duncan McKinley" he informed me, and just in case I wasn't aware about babies and the role of the male of the species in its procreation he added helpfully "He's a guy," and then more helpful still, 'And he's actually just retired.'

Very quickly I realised that the stories of the chaotic nature of the education system that we had been warned about in Jordanhill Teacher Training College may have had some kernel of truth in them. And that was even then before the system went mental to the power bonkers.

It does beg the question that before his retirement was Duncan McKinley ever 'with child' or am I just making these assumptions?

Maybe this was a vision into the future and self-identification gender altering etc. Who knows?
But one thing is certainly true. Mr. John McDonald, what a truly great bloke he was (and I'm sure he still is but he's long retired. (Update: - He very sadly passed away quite recently)) He then introduced me to the next character in this merry tale.

Because, you see, the next educational interaction I had was with the Principal Teacher of the maths department, Mr. Arthur Dixon himself, a legend in his own lunchtime and a person who was going to remain a good friend many years later.

Given this was two or three days into the teacher's new year when happiness is not at its greatest, his positivity was immense and massively reassuring.

'Ah brilliant. You're male', he said to me at the bottom of the stairs, again, another who unfathomably for me, was seemingly obsessed with my apparent masculinity.

'Do you play football?' he added, giving me a good insight into what suggested his priorities might be.

'Errrr, Nothing serious but I'll give it a go' I replied, and to be honest, I was loving the way this was heading.

"Smashing" beamed Arthur and we headed up the stairs. "By the way, have you got a permanent contract sorted yet?"

"Eh?"

And with that my fate was sealed. We got to the top of the stairs. I was briefly introduced to whoever was in the staffroom or at the landing at the top, a timetable was issued and off I trundled to Room 13!!!

Room 13. Unlucky for some.
But not for me.

I bloody loved it!

3 THE TIMES THEY ARE A CHANGIN'

Let's have a little bit of background information for any younger readers here.

The year was 1989. Life was a lot different back then.

There was no internet - computers themselves were just the famous BBC microcomputers (what happened to them then?), there were no mobile phones either as I think Yuppies were still to see the advantages of carrying a brick that weighed a kilogram with an antenna that you could hang a jacket on.

Also, the Iron Curtain still existed, and the Berlin Wall was still intact, so we were at war with the Russians and supported that dodgy geezer Osama Bin something or other; countries with names like Bosnia, Serbia and Croatia were comparatively unheard of since WW1.

South Africa was still an evil country where black people kept having terrible accidents on police staircases and where of course, sadly, the great Nelson Mandela was still locked up.

British Gas heated your home and SSEB got you plug loads of electricity.

Phones had something to do with the GPO but no one knew what it stood for.

Things were much cheaper back then too; indeed, the cost of food was just under £1 a pint.

America had some nutter running it then as well, so I suppose some things haven't really changed if I'm brutally honest.

Apparently Jive Bunny – Swing the Mood was number 1 in the charts for the whole of August but as you'll find out as you read this, that I probably didn't even realise that this was the case.

There were also only the two sexes in those days i.e., men and women albeit allowing for maybe a few poor hermaphrodites etc. and illnesses around the time mainly consisted of things like mumps, measles, chicken pox etc. you know, proper illnesses, with stress and anxiety being something you usually dealt with without having to give them all these fancy names that they do nowadays.

It was the ozone and AIDs rather than global warming which were the issues of international concern and diets were only for fat people.

Also, very significantly, Scotland at this time hadn't embarked on the four yearly self-flagellation process of finding the most idiotic 126 buffoons in the country, parking them in the ugliest building in the beautiful city of Edinburgh and getting them to ruin everything they put their grubby hands on.

So now that you've got your time bearings, that was the world back then, but now, follow me and I'll take you up to the staffroom.

4 THE STAFFROOM

The staffroom. Well, the one at the top on the left anyway.

Apparently there used to be male and female staff rooms way back many years ago. This gradually changed over the years and in this case became the smoking and non-smoking staff rooms. The top right staffroom was the smoking room when I started. In those days many teachers smoked, especially the female teachers, so the room we used (the non-smoking one) really only had four or five regular patrons with the other staff rooms being distributed around the school.

The motley crew of the mis-named Gents staff room consisted of the following: -

The already mentioned Mr Arthur Dixon, the Principal Teacher, ex Queens Park footballer and singer extraordinaire. There was always something about him which reminded me of Francis Rossi out of Status Quo. His jokes and his music that is. Not his football, he was absolutely superb. More of that later.

Next in line the much-travelled Assistant Principal Mr Bob Johnston, ex-mercenary soldier, gym aficionado and speaker of copious amounts of common sense. On occasion!

I wonder how many people know that he was at one time a cowboy model for a South African comic. Honestly.
No idea what it was called possibly something along the lines of Buffalo Bob and his Battle with the injun Talking Bull. But as it was in Afrikaans, it could have said anything.

Bob's a personal hero of mine, he figures in the tale later many times but that's all you really need to know for now. He's the guy that this book is basically a tribute to, so it follows that: -

    A- It's got to be good.

    B- You **have** to like it!!

Also, in the department in those days was Mr Bill Hughes - Mr Shoes / Shoesy / or even Elvis to the pupils. Bill was a nice guy, totally bonkers and mad as a box of frogs, but a nice guy, nonetheless. Bizarrely he had a tremendous ability to predict the weather, I mean seriously this guy could predict rain or snow on a sunny day almost to the exact minute and as this was pre smart phones and weather apps etc. it was a really useful and often very welcome attribute.

Then there was Mr G. Yes, Mr Galletly who was a Modern studies teacher.
He is a Rangers fan.
He is definitely not a Celtic fan.
Oh no no no...
He reminded everyone of this on a daily basis.
He used to address Arthur every morning on his arrival with 'Morning Commander.'

To this day none of us, including Arthur himself, have any idea who this commander is that he referred to at the start of each day.

However, I liked him, and he was what you might call an acquired taste.

He thought he looked like Richard Gear.

He didn't.

He must have had a tad of OCD as his actions when he came into the staffroom were always exactly the same.

Put bag on seat.
Remove locker key.
Open locker.
Remove cup.
Walk to sink.
Wipe cup with paper towel.
Walk back to locker.
Put cup back in locker.
Pick up bag and leave.

He did this exact routine every single day without fail.

Like Shoesy - he too was as mad as a wagonload of monkeys- but he was also a lot nicer than he let on.

And then of course there was my good friend Mr Peter (Pan) Murray. English teacher and a genuine total 100 per cent legend; his extremely loose morals will come up throughout this tale without a doubt. Still to this day he is one of my really good mates. However, that's the last good bit I'll say about him. He wouldn't have it any other way of course.

He is also famous for his extremely ……………………………………… Nah. Let's not go there.

So on to the very first class I taught.

5 FIRST CLASS

I can actually remember my very first class. Perhaps everyone does. They were a mixed ability S2 class. For reference this is approximately equivalent to a modern-day Higher class.
They worked on an individual based learning system called SMP. It had its flaws but essentially it was quite a good system.

Pupils seemed to be far more robust, mature, and capable in those days so I'm not sure if it would work nowadays but it was a really good way of pupils covering a suitable array of topics to a more than decent standard.

Basically, the class just taught themselves as they worked through the books, but all had roles like collecting homework sheets, making sure there were stocks of everything etc.
The teacher's role was to manage and administer the system and help with the individual difficulties as they arose. It actually worked pretty well. It was an absolute breeze to run too.

After about five minutes I was sorted and as far as the kids were concerned the clown who was not much older than them to be fair, in the double-breasted suit at the front of the class, had just more or less seemingly always been there.

Probation.

No, that system hadn't been introduced yet.

In at the deep end.

Sink or swim.

Spare the rod.

We liked our cliches too in those days!!

I think the period two class after that were meant to be nutters, but I got on with them ok.

That's a thing I've found over the years, that NEDs (non-educated delinquents), old ladies and dogs have always been surprisingly keen on me.

Well, I won a watch there, eh?

However, I reckon that if you follow that logic to its natural conclusion, then that woman who was in the news a couple of years back, firstly for selling drugs and then more positively for chasing paedophiles from the Raploch estate in Stirling, well if she had a couple of pit bulls or something, I'm sure she would find me like some kind of crack cocaine or the like.

Not to be sniffed at!!

Anyway, it was over quite quick, so it was along to the staffroom for the break.

6 THE MORNING INTERVAL

The normal morning interval routine went something like this.

Bell goes.
There are now 600 seconds (10 minutes) until it goes again. #
Meant to be back to meet class at door.
Yeah right.

Mad dash along corridor.

Hurl any lingering pupils out of the way. Needs must etc.
Race upstairs two at a time.
Visit to loo, which was conveniently placed at top of stairs, an option if required.

Sandwiches and snack - ok play piece - taken out of bag as greater than 80% of lunch eaten now is advisable so as not to interfere with lunchtime football; we had priorities you see.

Coffee? Recipe one teaspoon of instant coffee.

(Rule of coffee purchase. Spend as little as possible on maximum size jar. Quality and taste not an issue. I think back in 1989 we all chucked a couple of quid in each, bought a jar that when empty we could have lived in and that was us sorted for the next five years or so.)

Lob coffee into mug. It is a personal choice if you insist on mug being clean.
Fill cup to brim with boiling water and toxic rust particles from ancient urn. Helped with our iron intake.
Scald mouth with this muck but in later years learn to appreciate how vital it is to help with the process of staying awake or for limiting effects of hangover.
Remember, back in those days many times I, along with Peter and sometimes even Bob, was in work having been the victim of a mugging by the bar staff of some West end hostelry the night before.
We will leave it at that. Use your imagination. But this concoction was almost lifesaving at times.

Next, watch Arthur (like Mr. G, also a Rangers fan) read the back of Peter's Daily Record otherwise known then as the 'other' Rangers news. This may have already been read by Arthur during registration but was indeed read again as if it had been magically updated in the last two hours or so and always read from the back in the way towards the front of course. This allowed him to ignore all of the drivel they printed which was all found in the front and middle.
Come to think of it, I'm not sure that I ever saw Peter actually get to read his own paper in all the years we were there.

Bill would hide behind his Glasgow Herald no doubt scouring the weather forecasts for mistakes and apart from that first day Bob, Peter and I would each indulge in an obscene number of our favourite fruit. The banana.

Yes, the three of us over the years spent vast quantities of time and money on the three B's, that's birds, booze, and bananas.

And yes, just like Georgie B, we figured the rest we just wasted.

By the way, I've often wondered if we had eaten say, peaches, if the Windward Islands economy would have collapsed. We seriously went through hundreds of the bloody things.

Anyway. 600 seconds later. Run back to class.

No kids at door.

Period three - non contact.

Bastard!!!

Note to self. Learn the bloody timetable.

This has now been increased to 15 minutes. At time of writing it remains the only improvement in Scottish Education that I can actually think of.

7 THE REST OF THE DEPARTMENT

So far, we've met Arthur, Bob and Bill from the maths department but there were four others too.

Ms. Isobel Slack was a very nice lady who I think must have been a primary teacher at one time.

She was entirely age-blind in that she treated everybody in each of her classes as if they were the same age. Unfortunately for the secondary pupils, that age was about six years old. The kids always moaned about it, but I always suspected she was doing it to wind them up.

Put it this way, it certainly worked.

Her approach was along the lines of "Have you got a wee pencil there or do you want me to lend you one" and "Be a good girl and put it back in the jar when you're finished with it." Any of you who are currently teachers will realise that this has now become the norm in recent years but at the time it was considered quite eccentric and unusual.

There was Mrs Susan Dickie, a tremendous individual and one of those people that everybody just really likes. In later years I was to teach her son Michael, a brilliant guy (he was in the best class I ever taught, and these guys will definitely feature later, it's a good story, keep reading) and also her grandson.

There was also Miss Lesley Hall, still a maths teacher in those days but who would eventually go on to run the computing department of the future.

Computing as far as I was concerned was basically about logic and problem solving using BASIC or FORTRAN and it did link in quite well with the maths courses we had at the time.

Lesley was incredibly neat and well organised but gradually she saw the light and her connections to maths reduced.

Eventually she even had to change her name.
But that was only because she got married.

But out of the four, my absolute favourite was Mrs Kathleen Cornwell.

What can I say about Kathleen? Well for a start I'd be a lot quieter than her in doing it.

Jeez she was loud. I reckon she could easily and comfortably out-shout Brian Blessed.

Kathleen was from the island of Islay - that's the small piece of land west of the Tarbert peninsula where the whisky grows or something!! - and several years later I was to become friends with a lot of guys from that terrific island. All that time later they all knew and remembered her and her husband fondly.

I think in one case one guy's ears were/are still ringing!

I swear if the wind was blowing in the right direction, you could hear her from the Erskine bridge.

Don't get me wrong. Some people shout to control the class, some shout in frustration. I daresay some shout out of love.

But Kathleen was probably just born with massively overdeveloped vocal cords, and lungs to match, so she just yelled as a routine.

Come to think of it, I can't actually recall her ever being angry at all. She was just too nice and genuinely very caring. I loved her.

What a fantastic lady.

Four brilliant people. I can honestly say it was a genuine privilege to work with all of them.

8   IN THE BEGINNING

Over the years people have often asked how I got into teaching. I like to think they mean that since I've got such an unconventional approach to the job and don't buy any of the leftie theories that I must therefore be something of an imposter.

They're probably right.

I probably am.

I've tested what people really think, how much they believe and how far I can stretch the truth. Several times pupils have asked why I became a maths teacher. I've developed this little response, and this is what I tell them. It goes something like this...

I tell them that I used to be a joiner for the council. Ok, well one day I was fixing the floor in Room 7 (note, the secret to a good fake story is to give lots of pedantic detail and if possible, look them in the eye and nod regularly. You should try it; it works a treat. I'll teach you how as we go along.)

Anyway, one day I was fixing the floor in room 7, you remember the floor was quite new, yes? (It wasn't but they lap it up if you sell it properly.) Well, the head of maths sent a couple of miscreants in as they were not behaving elsewhere.

I was waiting for the glue to dry as you do, and you know how you've got to get it totally dry before you can cut the edges (yeah? nod etc.), so I got chatting to the two kids who, to be fair to them, actually seemed ok to me. We got chatting about their work and I was actually able to help them with it because I knew a bit of maths.

Anyway, the boss comes back in and seems really chuffed that the two guys have returned to their no doubt Oxbridge bound journey.

He asked me if he could send a few more and of course I agreed.

Turns out I was there for the week and since it was the council, I was able to drag out the job for two weeks. Could have been three but I didn't want to kick the arse out of it.

They had to get some kind of insurance for me to be in the room alone with the two boys, but it was easier just to put me on the temporary supply list.

Paid for two jobs. Ya dancer!!

After I had done it solid for six days the council were obliged to give me a short-term supply contract and it was just cheaper overall if they stopped paying me for the flooring work.

And there you have it. No degree, no training, nothing. I'm suddenly a respectable maths teacher.

Now this story is entirely horse poo but if you tell it with a straight face and nod regularly like I said, people seem quite happy to accept it.

However, the reality of the maths element of my teaching career is also somewhat strange too. This is genuinely one hundred per cent what happened.

I turned up to do *Physics* at Jordanhill teaching college.

On the day I had my 'interview' which didn't really go beyond name, address, degree etc. well the guy asked if I minded him sticking me down for maths too. I think he had a quota to reach.

"Suppose so," I said. And that's it. The rest is history. Well, actually mathematics. Ha ha!

From memory I think it was coincidentally my birthday too.

Like many things in my life, I don't seem to have made too much of a conscious decision about something which would then massively affect me throughout my life. But that's just the way it goes sometimes.

I think it worked out well for me overall.

9 IT'S QUITE AN EASY JOB (REALLY?)

A lot of people nowadays make out that teaching is a particularly difficult skill to master. They come up with daft ideas and replace them with even dafter ones. These stupid ideas are called pedagogies.

I, along with many of my colleagues, strongly suspect that the people who come up with these 'pedagogies' - honest, it's a real word - found the very basic 'art' somewhat challenging.
So, what does teaching really involve?

Let's think about it.

You (the teacher) know things.
The pupils in front of you don't know these things.
You tell them these things.

That's it.

It's really not rocket science.

Anyway, I found it quite straightforward and seemingly so did my classes. Very quickly my SMP individualised learning classes were fair battering through the course becoming dare I say it (oh dare dare!!!) confident individuals and successful learners as they get called nowadays. Everyone had various jobs and it was fair peachy running the class.

I had a decent range of classes too.

In S3 to S6 the classes were set according to ability and my third-year class was the second section, so we were doing the same as the top set but apparently had slightly less ability to do this work. The first chance to test how successful or not I may have been, came in the October of that year.

Ladies and Gentlemen, please be seated for the Credit Block One Test.

My class and the top section and possibly the third section too all set their individual abilities against this ferocious beast.

To be honest I was a little worried. Everything had been going absolutely smoothly and just far too well up to now, and I was just waiting for it all to go pear-shaped.

The morning of the test arrived and for the classes who were sitting said beast, the papers were issued row after row.

At this stage the panic began. The sweating followed. Fingernails were bitten down/up to the elbow.
And no doubt, the pupils were quite nervous too!!!

An hour or so later the papers were handed in and over the next day or so we as a department took to marking them.

At the end of this process the classes were realigned according to their newly proven mathematical ability.
Sadly, I lost about two thirds of my class.

'Aha' I hear the dear reader say. 'You messed it up right enough.'

Not so. Not at all so in fact.

It was only because they had done so well that they got moved, and moved indeed they were...into the top set.
I got all the ones who dropped down.

The new lot however were a cracking bunch, and a great time was had by all, but this was effectively my first educational test, and all was good.

The school seemed happy enough too as my contract got extended until Christmas. I like to think the two events were linked but as I said earlier, I'm not entirely sure education is as organised as that.

There was probably just no one else on the list at that time.

10 THE HEADIE

The Headmaster, when I arrived at the school was the legendary Mr James Colraine.

To say this man had a presence would be the understatement of the year. Staff and pupils alike feared him, but all respected him.

The male teachers were expected to always wear a jacket in the corridors and if he said jump your only concern related to the expected size of the gap between yourself and the ground.

There was one individual who never seemed bothered by him at all. Surprisingly, that was yours truly.

I thought he was great, absolutely brilliant.

For reasons I have never been able to fathom, he seemed to really like me.

When other staff were being growled at, I had his arm round my shoulder, with him asking me things like what I was up to at the weekend and if I was still seeing 'that wee bird' that he had seen me with one night when I bumped into him as I was heading into a pub.

For the record. No idea.

Perhaps he'd had a few!!

He seriously couldn't have been nicer or kinder to me and the following is a true story which I assume is safe to relate all these years later.

My contract had seemingly got extended again due to various promotions in the school and I was in the Academy until the summer. Still temporary but there for the whole year.

At that stage it was up to the council (Strathclyde Region as they were known then) as to if or where they would put me. Could be anywhere from Lochgilphead in the west to Coatbridge in the east or deepest darkest Ayrshire or even beyond I suspect.

Anyhow, Mr Colraine, (please note in writing this book I started to call him Mr. C but as I still have so much respect for him, I've gone back to calling him Mr Colraine and capital H for Headteacher too!!), anyway he called me into his office.

He explained there was a job in the maths department - *good* - but that it was open to everyone in SRC - *bad*.

"You know I'm allowed to recommend one temporary post to be made permanent in the school", he said.

I stared blankly, the significance of this message making me want to scream out but unable to respond. Fingers, toes etc. crossed and crossed again. I must have looked like some kind of rope to him.

"However, I'm sorry but there are thirteen people with longer service than you in the school," he continued.

My heart sank.

But not for long!

He smiled and looked at me over those big glasses of his and said "But, it's up to me, sooooooooooo I'm recommending YOU to be the one that gets kept on."

In my head it was a Joel Stransky drop goal in the Rugby World Cup final versus the All-Blacks moment, which hadn't actually happened at that point in time and indeed wouldn't for another five years. But in my head, I was celebrating, punching the air and sprinting back to the halfway line high-fiving Joost van der Westhuizen and Captain Francois Pienaar all the way.

In reality, my reaction whilst still being delighted and also slightly shocked, meant that it was probably a bit more sedate but nonetheless, I was totally ecstatic.

During that summer the permanent contract duly arrived and yours truly was made a permanent member of staff.

I was always thankful to that absolutely wonderful man. He really looked out for me. I still to this day have no idea what I did to deserve this massive courtesy, but I am truly grateful for it and I hope I repaid his trust.

To make an almost political point here, if there were more head teachers in the country, that were like Mr Colraine, an awful lot of society's problems would diminish rapidly. Just my opinion, but it's almost certainly correct.

I've have gone on to have quite a few 'headies' over the years, one or two really good including the really good one I currently work for, and there have been one or two embarrassingly awful ones too, but no one was quite as good as Mr Colraine.

At this point it's worth adding in that pretty much all senior managers have been really kind to me in all my years in Dumbarton, with one unnamed and obvious exception.
(Who's that then Mr.B. One day I'll tell you!!)

But, on the subject of Senior Managers, John McDonald that I talked about earlier definitely gets special mention too.

One Easter, my mate and I had gone on a trip to India.

We couldn't afford the regular Heathrow to Calcutta prices, so we had to travel el-cheapo class which meant some obscure Romanian airline with a stopover in Bucharest.
Unfortunately, it meant we also had to travel Monday to Monday which meant I would miss the first day back of the new term.

Bob and I arranged a cunning (pre internet, pre mobile phone) plan to get round this.

Bob would go in to work on the Monday and tell John that I had, in total panic, phoned him in the middle of the previous night from Bucharest airport, raising him from his deep slumber, and telling him our plane was massively delayed.

Well, accidents happen and all that.

So, that's what we did and no one, including John, ever mentioned the event after that.

All was good in other words.

However, many years later, on a DAMS night (Dumbarton Academy Men's Night) which was open to all by the way, I 'fessed up to John.
I told him the real story and how I had carried the burden of lying to him for all these years.

John said,' It's ok. I always knew you two were both at it.'

'Eh? How come?' I replied, quite shocked if truth be told.

'Oh, come on,' he continued, 'It had to be a figment of you two numpties' imagination. Come on. Seriously?'

'Anyway,' he added, 'Who in their right mind would be stupid enough to wake Bob Johnston in the middle of the night?'

Right enough. He's definitely got a point there.

11 COMIC RELIEF AND CHE GUEVARA… EAT YER HEART OUT

If I get away with this book, I'm going to publish the photos of that day. Here's why.

Ok, so schools have fun days, in fact, schools nowadays have a lot of fun days.

Sometimes money is raised for what are usually, not always in my opinion, but usually, good causes. Sometimes I do feel that the main reason for having these fun days is for photo opportunities and pictures for newsletters rather than to impart the values of altruism or to make pupils aware of how fortunate they are compared to many poor souls throughout the country and indeed the whole world.

I'm not really sure how getting your parents to donate a pound so that you don't have to wear a uniform really gives an insight into the real meaning of charity but there you go.

But as you've guessed, it was not always so.

Yes, at the good ship Dumbarton Academy in my first year of teaching we decided to give our support to what was at the time, a wonderful organisation, 'Comic Relief.'

That day we certainly did Lenny and Co proud.

No obligation was issued, and in those days, there was no school uniform anyway, so anyone wanting to take part really had to make the effort and actually dress up. I know nowadays 'dressing up' often just requires the purchase of a sometimes-dubious poor-quality, Chinese sweat shop manufactured, outfit purchased from Amazon, which is worn once and then immediately discarded. Ironic, especially if, as often is the case, there is an environmental element to the charity!!

Fortunately, that didn't seem to be the case in those days.

Essentially, costumes made by pupils and staff were created entirely from scratch. You will of course realise that the two words which stand out the most are the two most significant ones, 'and staff.'

Yes indeed, this was by any definition a joint effort between staff and pupils. As far as I recall, there were more people dressed up than not and the day seemed to develop its own feeling of organised chaos.

Now while there were the usual suspects in terms of costumes like cowboys, space aliens etc. there were a few that deserve special mention.

We had a rather 'naughty' schoolboy, you know the type, a 'Just William' lookalike in short trousers who somehow managed to get his shirt tail to surreptitiously hang out of his fly.

This was played by none other than Mr Arthur Dixon himself.

We also had, what can only be described as a 'gay sailor' represented by the legendary Mr Peter Murray. When I say gay sailor, it's not meant to be derogatory, it's just that I'm not sure how to describe hot pants and a sailor's hat any other way. The worst part of it were the knee length white socks which no doubt *had* come out of his closet.

Bob arrived in military fatigues. Some thought he was dressed 'in costume' as a soldier but a few of us knew the truth. Bob had indeed been a soldier but not the normal sensible organised regimental type.

No no, this was too soft for our Bobster.

Bob had genuinely been a mercenary soldier in the African jungle many years before and the small holes that could be seen in his suit weren't the results of moths or of poor-quality material that some of the staff and pupils suspected them to be.

These small holes were actually small bullet holes from some of his near misses in 'The Congo.'

Two things to add here about Bob.

He was by some distance the best teacher ever in Dumbarton Academy and the kids were simultaneously both terrified and extremely respectful of him.

Over the years I've bumped into many many former pupils and heard them say lots of things about him (always positive by the way), but their terror lay in their fertile imaginations about his past and the experiences they believed he had had.

I always laughed when I heard them telling me what they thought he had done and been involved in because it was invariably inaccurate or just plain wrong and also because I knew the real truth.

The truth was FAR worse.

And one other thing while we're on the subject. This bit is good. Bob's mercenaries back in the Congo were on the 'other side' fighting against Che Guevara's group, and although Bob admits that in hindsight, he had probably joined the wrong side, his choice was made by his group taking a more 'conventional' approach and paying more.

Mercenaries and principles, it's a bit of a grey area you see.

But, where it gets interesting, is that since Bob's side were the ones who won the various skirmishes, he really does quite legitimately feel very hard done to in that it should indeed be a picture of him rather than CG (that's Che Guevara not Colin Gellatly btw) who should be on tee shirts and posters adorning the walls of many student flats, probably even still to this day.

Peter, on the other hand, feels that he himself would have been better as a replacement for the tennis girl with the bare arse!!

Also, one other very significant character that definitely deserves mention that day was the wonderful Dougie MacIndoe, hero of the French department. In those days Doug was the absolute life and soul of the school, a tremendous guy and everyone just loved him.

Doug turned up, as only he could.... dressed as an African woman.

A 'big' African woman if you get my drift.

A 'big' African woman with a couple of large balloons down his top, well some African women do have huge knockers, don't they? He had also blackened his face and was wearing some sort of ridiculous wig.

I realise nowadays this would not be acceptable and there would be assertions of racism. Nothing could be further from the truth and bear in mind the various ethnicities of this author!! Of course, I'm biassed towards Doug but I've checked with African friends about it, and they all laugh out loud especially when they see the pictures.

Everyone found it hilarious. I know I certainly did.

And then there were the pupils.

We had just about anything you can imagine that day, even if the costume simply meant painting something daft across your face.

There were a lot of cheerleaders (mainly female) and several boys dressed as women, but I think my favourites were the 'Naughty Nun and the Pervy Priest', two girls going round the school dressed as men of the cloth and carrying a large bible.

Well, it said 'Bible' on one side but on closer inspection, the other side in large bold letters declared it to be the 'Joy of Sex'. These two carried this off brilliantly and to this day it is one of the best efforts at fancy dress I've seen.

Yours truly was dressed as a surgeon, they seemed to wear green in those days, though now it seems to be blue they cut about in. Anyhow with some fake blood and a large cardboard scalpel I felt I did my bit. I did feel a bit of an arse going home on the train that day dressed like that, but we raised plenty of dosh, the school felt like a really friendly community and a great time was had by all.

We also had a game of netball against the senior girls and though I can't remember the score, despite our endless cheating we were well trounced.

I feel in telling this part of the tale it gives you a right insight into what the school was like back in those days. In many ways it really was like a social friendship group and the simple fact that so many people were happy to make a complete fool of themselves indicates the lack of arrogance hanging around the place back then.

Did it make the local papers?

Well probably not, though when you step back and think about it, that may just have been a good thing.

12 JOHNNY GOLDENBALLS

At the top, or certainly very near the top of the Education tree of daftness, are a particular group of people who are known as the School Inspectors.

They are very nice people generally, perhaps only in that cuddly black mamba sort of way with some members of the staff, but in my dealings with them (thrice) I've always found them a fairly decent if not very useful bunch.

The fact that they represent and look for the exact opposite of what I believe in, makes this appraisal somewhat unlikely, but I do feel that way, nevertheless.

The reason for this probably goes back to my first experience of meeting these people.

In my second year of teaching, HMIE (Her Majesty's Inspectorate of Education) I assume or whatever they were called back in the day (BITD), duly announced that they were going to inspect the no doubt seemingly dodgy goings on at the Academy.

There were no great warnings from senior management that I can remember, there were no noticeable stresses on staff, pupils, and myself and generally we were almost blissfully unaware of these people visiting at all.

Well, we had nothing to worry about, did we?

And so, they arrived.

I assume also there was more than one but the only one I remember was a lady who was probably in her fifties, very well dressed and generally a decent sort all round.

She looked like how I imagine that school inspectors themselves imagine teachers to be like and almost certainly were, back when they themselves were pupils.

After a morning or so of meetings / deals / threats from the boss (Mr Colraine - yeah, like they stood a chance!!!) they visited various classes, asked the kids a few questions and just generally got the feel of what was going on.

No stress whatsoever at all.

But............................

I did manage to get myself noticed and not just once but twice.

Here's how it went.

The lady concerned, let's call her Anne, as I vaguely recall that being her name, or was it, Mary? A lot of Mary's seemed to be around in high educational positions. Especially in Dumbarton.

Perhaps her name was Mary. We'll call her Mary.

Anyway, she was the one tasked with checking out the maths and as it would happen, the English departments too.

In those days Peter, my good friend from the English department, was still a single(ish) sort of guy and having been inspected by our Lady, he had no doubt taken it upon himself to flirt and charm in his unique style as he did in an overtly over the top way to all womankind at any and every opportunity, whilst discussing any relevant after class issues.

Something must have happened anyway as immediately after seeing his class she came into mine not in a state of undress or anything silly but certainly well flustered and in a terrifically good mood.

The class I had that period were the 'Foundies'.

For all non-teachers who may read this book, there is an unwritten educational law of the universe that states that any time anyone of importance visits your class it has to be when your worst class is sitting in front of you.

Couldn't she have picked a more able class where she could see the pupils learn things.

No no no. Not the, by now, fourth year class all hurtling towards credit who, if you remember, had been relegated into my second class, or perhaps she could even have seen my Higher class. But no, of course that would have been far too easy.

Nope. She visited yours truly with his Foundie class.

Note to new teachers. Foundation is what the Scottish Government tell us, is the equivalent of a National 3 nowadays. That's total bollocks. It's not equivalent by a long chalk.

If you doubt this, go and get an old Foundation paper (preferably paper 2) and give it to your National 4 class.

And watch them weep.

But back to the Foundies.

They were an almost entirely male class.

(Please note: to avoid confusion with the current fad in education this means that almost all the pupils in the class were male, not that all of them were greater than 50% anatomically male!)

The Foundies weren't the best at maths, but the secret was to break the lesson down into two parts.

First, the maths bit involving fractions, decimals, percentages, and other assorted rubbish etc. and then the second part mainly football.

The split should probably be about 3 to 1 but ours was seldom breaching 1 to 3.

A foundy class in those days could tell the difference between the two.

Could your Nat 4 class do this?

Come to think of it. Could your Nat 5 class even do this?

Hmmmmm. I don't think so.

Anyway, we worked our lesson through whatever boring arithmetic we were dealing with at the time, and as is always the case with pupils of that level, if they put in an effort then they coped more than easily and as this great bunch were quite keen for me to look good in front of Mary (Anne? /Mary? Yeah, we settled on Mary, didn't we?), well they therefore just battered through the work but far too quickly for the lesson to last a whole period unfortunately.

I really liked them and as arrogant as it sounds, I think the feeling was mutual, luckily for me.

So, what happened. Of course, we ran out of work far too quickly.

Panic set in.

Remember in those days you didn't really plan lessons as such. They just sort of took care of themselves. You basically formed the general premise in your mind in the time it took them to arrive, and you just had a vague idea of what you wanted them to know. Then you taught it.

And it worked!

But this time what it meant was that I had run out of any 'planned material.'

Fortunately, at that point I remembered I had my individualised learning that I had set up for the class. This was really just a poorly made-up version of what S1 and S2 were doing. Nothing special, just a list of textbooks and pages in a format like an excel spreadsheet which of course, had yet to be invented.

The pupils took different textbooks and did small pieces of separate topics in various orders that sort of helped them with the course. I recorded their progress on my pre-excel spreadsheet. I wonder if there was a relative of Mr. Gates in that class. Hmmm.

Anyway, it was only really there so that if I got bored out of my mind with the work, I could fob them off with this, as remember, individualised learning was a breeze to run but wow, Mary absolutely loved it. I was the best thing since sliced bread and she was delighted.

I was perhaps what they nowadays call, 'sector leading'.

But she didn't tell *me* this. Instead, she told Bob who was acting head of the department during those few weeks as Arthur had scarpered to some other role purely coincidentally at the exact same time as the inspectors were due in the school. Only joking, he had a temporary promotion and other roles to be responsible for.

Well, I got slagged something rotten by Bob and the rest of the department.

'What a wonderful young man'

'What a caring teacher'

'What a phenomenal individual and no doubt gifted and gentle lover'.

Well perhaps not the last one but you get the picture.

Bob summarised this to everyone at the feedback session after the next departmental meeting and this led to my nickname becoming Golden Balls.

And then all was fine once more, that is, until I lost my wallet.

And guess who found it? No, not Mary the inspector, but one of our cleaners. This lovely person (all our cleaners are lovely people, it's like another rule of the teaching universe) felt that the wallet should only be opened in the presence of more than just herself for security reasons, so sods law had it that the inspector was the one who opened my wallet.

And so, she did.

A second or so before the condom fell out.

That bastard Bob Johnston then changed his nickname for me.

That bastard Bob Johnston then renamed me 'Johnny' Golden Balls.

13 ROOM THIRTEEN

My room when I first went to the school was, as I've said earlier, Room 13. It was upstairs in the old part of the school, and I believe at one point the corridor may have been exposed to the elements, but by the time I was there it had been enclosed with glass panels with some sort of wire grid inside the glass.

Classy. Which it should be in a school.
Get it?
Classy.

In the winter it could get mighty cold in that corridor.
But if you weren't triskaidekaphobic and were brave enough to venture inside, it was an Aladdin's cave of nonsense and gibberish.

It had cupboards galore which may well have been antiques and for which none of the keys matched the locks. There were massive radiators ON THE BLOODY WALL, sorry; an explanation of why this has to get mentioned will happen later in the section about the 'New School'; and it had the requisite massive board, as in those days writing on a board was still quite rightly considered a viable method of teaching rather than learning through the medium of dance/ mime/ or some other trendy crap as is now often encouraged.

It also had a sink.

Why? Well, like many things in my life, I have a theory.

I've always let kids go to the toilet when they ask. Some of the classroom fascists make an issue of this but it's never bothered me.
That said if a pupil endlessly asked out (and it was worth checking if it was bang on the hour or half past etc.) when they were no doubt meeting up with pals I used to wait until a genuine opportunity arose and after 'temporarily' refusing the pupils request to leave the room, yes, you've guessed it, on went the taps.

A minor form of torture being supplied by the council. It was almost compulsory to use it. Watching the pupil squirm, a little cruel perhaps. But it amused me.

The sink was also useful for clearing up the blood. But we should probably just scuttle quickly by this bit.

The council must have had a job lot of mustard, brown and blue paint as those were the main colours in the school at the time. Mine was light blue at the top and dark blue at the bottom, coincidentally the same colours as my first car (a Mark II Escort that did 0 - 60 in ………. the summer.
And funnily enough, just like my classroom, it also had a brown door.)

Around the classroom were the various folders containing the SMP individualised learning books.

These books, by the way, had names like Turning, Travelling Around and Speed which led to Arthur's endless jokes which he only ever repeated a thousand times or so...

Pupil: I've finished Travelling Around
Arthur: Where did you go?

Pupil: I've finished Turning
Arthur: Did it make you dizzy?

Pupil: I've done Speed
Arthur: Druggy bastard, report to the office.

The last one of course I made up, but you get the picture. Arthur was a big fan of 'Carry On' films and the like, as I'm sure you're not remotely surprised to find out.

Anyway, that was my room and gradually I decorated it with all sorts of daft stuff, and I made sure to avoid these stupid posters that maths teachers usually put up showing you what a bloody circle or a triangle looks like.

No, my room was class.

I even had a picture of that famous mathematician Wendy James out of Transvision Vamp on the wall and to give the room a bit of culture there was a poster with a, vouched for by Bob, African proverb: -

*Until the lions have their own historians,
Tales of hunting will always glorify the hunter.*

Pretty clever stuff, eh? Sadly, so true nowadays.

Now as I've also already said, the SMP individualised learning books were distributed around the folders pinned to the wall.

So, one day, one young urchin, let's call him William, comes out and says.
"Sorry Sir, I've done the wrong book".
"What book have you done?" I enquired.
"Err sorry Sir, I've done Speed".
"Ya useless druggie etc. etc.", I could have said but of course didn't. What I did say was "What's wrong with that?"
"It's just that Sir, and really sorry about this Sir, it's just that I appear to have done errrrr, what seems to have been the answer book."

Funny thing was, it wasn't even correct.

I suspect he ended up designing the new school.

One other thing to mention about that wonderful room was the desks. The desks were brilliant. Thirty-two tables, not one of which matched or fitted together as the ones that did went to more senior members of staff.
I didn't mind this if truth be told. In fact, I fully welcomed the pecking order and the 'serving your time' idea.
I think it's sad disappearance in recent years is proving disastrous for schools but that's a discussion for another time.

Anyway, the desks were wooden and by wooden, I mean softwood.

You know the sort. The perfect consistency - (is that the right word?)- for gouging out a name or a piece of graffiti.

There was a lot of abuse on these desks that I inherited. A lot of questions unfortunately asked about the possibility of intercourse with the Pope if you get my drift, and the usual obsession with male genitalia, but my favourite piece of vandalism was relatively new and obviously must have been created since my arrival at the school.

You knew you had arrived in the Academy when your own parentage was questioned in a visible case of tabletop unpermitted creationism, so of course I absolutely loved the 'Bhattacharyya is a Bast' message that was left for me.
That is exactly what it said.

'Bhattacharyya is a Bast'

I absolutely loved the fact that my name being so long, it didn't give the poor wretch enough space to finish the abusive message and also that somewhat bizarrely they had taken the time to spell my name one hundred per cent correctly.

You see, in Dumbarton, even the neds have some class.

Anyway, I kept that table at the back of my classroom even when we were supplied with new desks which did match and did join together. I felt it was a sort of badge of honour.

After the first summer I got moved downstairs to Room 9, as room 13 became our base, but Room 9 downstairs my friends, was very conveniently positioned right next door to the one and only Mr. Bob Johnston!!

14   USEFUL IN-SERVICE?

In Service days take place five times a year.
I think the unions negotiated them as a way to annoy teachers as they seem to hate us even more than a lot of the general public do sadly.

These special child free days are often just basically an opportunity for idiots to compete for promotion in a 'Who's got the daftest idea we can come up with today' type of game.

Seriously the amount of crap and nonsense I've heard over the years at these things defies belief.

It's not as if it's even an interesting type of crap and nonsense that I just disagree with or have a different opinion on, it's just garbage.

These people really need to get out into the real world and see what's going on.

And they also need to learn how to present.

How embarrassing the whole 'computer/projector malfunctions' are. Red writing on a blue background or yellow on white. What idiot came up with those combinations?

And then it's all about excuses.

No one is thick anymore. They have one of 241 made up illnesses - maths anxiety, that's one of the latest belters by the way. The presentation is made by either someone on the up in the school who admits later it's all nonsense or they bring in some badly dressed pongo who heads up some publicly funded excuse group to tell you why Mungo Johnny can't be expected to sit for more than three minutes without his human rights being breached, or they use yet another version of the 'Twinkie' defence.

But it's all about Teaching and Learning of course!!! As if no one ever knew this before.
They even have committees with that as their heading by the way.

Someone must have come up with this. Probably at Social Service headquarters deep down in some extinct volcano...

'I say Tarquin, if you're not overly stressed could you please tell us about that new initiative you were going to foist on those bloody teachers'.

'Ah yes Julia dahling, I suggest we ban them from doing anything that would benefit any hard-working kids, cause you know I'm worried that us and our hanger on buddies in the HQ might get found out'.

'Top idea, I need to keep this overpaid job dahling, might struggle to get another with my sociology degree'.

'Yes, well let's get them to set up Teaching and Learning groups as a distraction'.

'Good stuff, perfect balance of pointlessness and patronising!'

Anyway, you get the idea.

I must have been to over a hundred of these.

Only two good things stand out.

Years ago, we had one visitor. He stood up and addressed us like this:-

"I'm a sure the first thing you're a wondering is a where I getta theees aaaaccent", he informed us.

It sounded somewhat familiar, but it was hard to immediately place in the context of an in-service day.

"If I tell you I a-have to be a-home before the a sun rises", he continued.

Well bite me! The guy was from Transylvania.

Yes, he could have been a voice double for The Count from Sesame Street. Top bloke, I could have listened to him all day.

He was terrific.

Cannot for the life of me remember what he was talking about, mind, but what a guy?

When my own kids were young and watching Sesame Street, whenever I heard, 'One pretend a sheep, Two pretend a sheep' I always thought of that guy.

The only other useful thing I learned from all of these In-Service days was this. Feel free to take it onboard and use yourself. In fact, please stick it down as CPD (Continuous Personal Development.)

Well as you may or may not know they sometimes give you a scone on the morning of these in-service days but unfortunately you can never spread the butter as it's straight out of the fridge and rock solid. Well, here's what you do to overcome the distressing situation.

1. Lift tea/coffee cup off of saucer.

2. Place butter on saucer.

3. Place cup back down over butter.

4. Cut scone in half and open jam.

5. Clean up inevitable scone crumbs carnage.

6. Lift cup. The timing of this operation allows the butter to now be perfectly spreadable.

In twenty-five years or so which equates to somewhere around 130 of these In-service punishment days, that literally is the only decent part and certainly the most useful thing I've learned.

15 A CHRISTMAS TALE

I hope dear readers that you are enjoying this book so far and that you are building up a little bit of a picture of what teaching was like back in the eighties and in this case the nineties. Here's another entirely true tale.

If it seems far-fetched, I genuinely am very sorry, but this is once again, without a word of a lie, exactly what actually happened on the day.
(Allegedly of course)

Each year in Dumbarton Academy we would have a Christmas lunch just before the Christmas holiday.

This of course is the period from the time towards the end of December to the first week or so of January which is often now strangely and unnecessarily referred to as the Winter holiday.

It's Christmas by the way, my Muslim friends tell me to say this to everyone on their behalf!!

Please note, in some departments (which an unnamed colleague jokingly refers to as the lesser academic subjects,) the Christmas / Winter holiday extends from early November and finishes shortly before Easter, but each to their own.)

Well anyway, at this lunch before the food was partaken of, we had a Secret Santa.

The procedure was that Arthur, who, you remember, was my boss, in the weeks before this date, had made a list of all the staff and wrote each person's name on a small piece of paper which then got folded up and dropped into his tin. He went round all the staff and each person took a piece of paper from his tin and when they opened it up secretly, that was the person that they were to buy a gift for. You know the sort of thing. Basic stuff.

All the gifts were left with Arthur who in many ways was Santa's behind the scenes little helper. He brought all the gifts down to the hall on the day and organised everything. He did a great job of it too.

Each year one member of the staff would dress up as Santa himself and distribute the presents at the lunch with Arthur cracking jokes at everyone's expense with the microphone. What I do need to point out is that he was aided by the local minister. A Man of the cloth.

Well, this one year, your's truly became the Dumbarton Academy staff 'Santa'. I had a wonderful 'elf' helping me as well in the one and only Rona Evans.

(Big praise to the people who named the games hall after her, years later when she passed away, years too early. I always thought that was a magnificent gesture. Thankyou from me personally and almost certainly on behalf of all her friends.)

Anyway, back to the tale and all was fine and dandy.

Arthur would draw a present from the bag and read out the name.

He would pass it to the minister.

The minister would pass it to Santa and Santa would deliver.

After about ten minutes or so of this, all was still running perfectly smoothly. Name after name. Cheeky comment from Arthur as and when appropriate. Minister enjoying the banter, that sort of thing, you get the drift.

Until my own name got read out.

The minister handed me my present which was obviously some kind of magazine.

Thinking nothing of it I accepted it from said man of the cloth. Unfortunately, as he got it out of the bag it got snagged and had begun to tear just as he handed it to me.

There's a kind of obligation to open it then and there, with everyone watching, but I quickly realised I couldn't, without causing some serious concern.
'Why was this?' you may ask.

Well, somewhat fortuitously, I inadvertently got a quick peek through the tear in the paper and what confronted me was a rather pert bare backside and also the top of a suspender belt. The minister smiled, knowingly it seemed, whilst I just withered.

To be honest, if he had seen it then he certainly didn't let on.

'This month's edition of The Economist,' I think I mumbled as I hurriedly tried to refold the paper and hide Penthouse December Nineteen Ninety something under my arm.

I had to wedge it between the coat and my fake beard and walked around holding it unnecessarily tightly whilst giving out the rest of the presents as I didn't dare put it down or have someone helpfully look after it for me.

I must have looked as if I had had a stroke or something.

The next fifteen minutes or so of doing the deliveries became a bit of a blur as the wrapping paper gradually started to tear and by the end had almost fallen off. Fortunately for me however no one saw what it really was, being too distracted with their own gifts. It didn't help that my bloody 'elf' assistant kept trying to 'helpfully' grab the magazine off me as she could see I was struggling.

Now to me it was quite obvious who had got my name out the tin.

It was my good and dear friend Mr John Christie, the techie teacher. File under Genuine and Legend. And complete Bastard!

John was one of my really good mates in the school. We played football every day except Fridays when he and I used to go to the pub at lunchtime. In the afternoon I taught calculus to the higher maths class, he played about with band saws, chisels, nail guns and the like. Mental!! This does appear to be a key trait of technical staff or so it seems. In fact, it is often alleged that Techie departments are where escapees from the French Foreign legion go 'to forget.'

But, to get back to the story, as all you good readers know, revenge is a dish best served cold.

This expression, which, like many other delightful turns of phrase is probably Shakespearean, basically means do it after a period of time when the bastard's not expecting it.

Well, it was definitely going to be my dish and twelve months was the period of hypothermic ambient temperature before I got John back.

But when I did, I got him good! In fact, it was more than good!! It was wonderful, a thing of great beauty.

What happened was this. The following year I went to Arthur and told him my plan. Basically, to start with, I just needed John's name out the tin, so a bit of cheating was involved. Arthur had no qualms about this at all and indeed helped me open all the names until we found John's.

I meanwhile purchased a porn mag from the newsagents at Thornwood roundabout and wrapped it up with John's name on the gift tag.

'So what?' you may say. That's exactly the same as what he did.

Well, it wasn't quite!! Let's just say that this was a magazine that was probably of more interest to members of the gay male community. It was called Euroboys or something similar.

Aha!! So now it gets a bit more interesting, doesn't it?

The day arrives and again Santa (who this year is being played by someone else) is merrily handing out the presents.

John Christie's name duly gets called.

Santa delivers.

John opens his parcel (but by now I'm starting to have doubts as to whether this was perhaps such a good idea after all.)

Remember, although we live in bonkers times nowadays where this would probably be categorised somehow as a hate crime, which it most certainly was not, even back in those days the distribution of pornography in a school was probably not something that was likely to be seen as a priority in a school development plan.

Anyway, worried I should not have been.

Not a jot.

John rips open the paper and when he sees what it is he does two things.

He first of all laughs really loud, I mean seriously bellowingly loud and standing up points over at me waving the magazine shouting 'that was you ya b**%$rd wasn't it.'

He's a subtle chap!!

But secondly, and this is the good bit, he shows the magazine to all the women at his table who at first are shocked, then pretend to be disgusted, but then seem to quickly overcome their shock and disgust as they start to squabble over the magazine all the while desperately searching in their handbags trying to find their reading glasses to get the best view. 'Ooo that's shocking, look at the size of that, get it over here' etc. etc.

To be honest they were all terrific sports about it.

But it was Dumbarton. No one was meant to be offended and no one was. In fact, a great time was had by all. John and I still remain very good friends to this day.

Footnote to this tale:

I've mentioned that we played football most lunchtimes.

Well one of the guys who played was John's boss. His name was Gus, another great guy.
In fact, come to think of it all techie teachers seem pretty good sorts, it's like yet another rule of the teaching universe, you never seem to get a bad one, all great, all dead friendly, all nuts in my experience. I think it's the wood fumes that causes this.

Well, when Gus was in having his shower after the game, John quietly slipped the Euroboys magazine into Gus's kit bag. Gus dumped his dirty kit in on top and didn't notice the male pornographic extravaganza. The first person who actually did notice it was Gus's wife when she went to put his kit in the wash.

What a woman, what a star. What she did was brilliant. She just left it under his pillow which he only found when he went to bed that night.

Rumour is she is alleged to have turned to him and asked him if he still found her attractive!

16 SILVERMINTS, TAYTO CRISPS, AND WHY YOU DON'T MESS WITH THE IRISH

I have had many good classes over the years but one class in particular stands out. These guys were simply class. They were all brilliant fun and the kind of people you genuinely found you wanted to be around. It was not a chore at all to teach these guys.

Well in this class there was a relatively new girl, and she was from Ireland.

Like the rest, she was very clever, worked very hard and enjoyed the 'craic' as she would call it.

Thus, I took it as given that it was compulsory for me to rip it out of her accent as much as possible.

Ah grand!

To be sure!

Go on go on! (Father Ted was becoming very popular around that time too you see.)

But before I tell this tale I really don't want you to get the wrong idea that 'yer woman the blonde girl' was in any way being bullied by me. It was teasing.
How do I know?

Well reason one, it was usually her who started it if I didn't have the decency to take the initiative to rip it out of her accent, and also, because she laughed too, all the time.

Teasing rather than bullying equals fun.

Reason two, I was her supplier of Silvermints and Tayto crisps which I brought back from my many trips in those days to the Emerald Isle.

Well one day, she was about to answer some question and I said something cheeky in my own heavy version of Dublinese and so she quite rightly decided to take me on.

'Mr B. Sure Yer always taking the Mick outta me sor. It's terribly unfair, sure I'm gonna report ya' and although I knew she was joking she was, in fairness, absolutely correct.

So, in front of everybody I apologised. 'I'm really sorry, it's unprofessional, I know. You are absolutely correct; I promise not to do it again' I said.

"Well sure now sir that's allroight, we've got that sorted but as long as that's the last we hear of it we'll say no more about it."

She then engaged in much finger wagging etc. etc.

So what?

Well sometimes fate plays right silly buggers.

I looked at the actual question she was about to answer, it must have been something along the lines of $2\frac{1}{6}$ plus $1\frac{1}{6}$.

In case you haven't worked out where the punchline is coming from you add the whole numbers first giving you three then you add the ⅙ and its partner ⅙. This adds to give you two sixths which in turn when you simplify it leaves you with ⅓ and put together gives you 3⅓ which given how smart this class were they all spotted the answer immediately and knew what was about to happen.

Probably because she had been distracted, and so before I could stop her, she shouted out "The answer's tree and a turd sor"

There was much uproar.

I'm sure she has grown up to be an incredible young woman, no doubt at all about that, and there are definitely many more tales to tell from that superb class. As I said earlier, a brilliant bunch of pupils.

17   SPAIN – THANK GOD THERE WERE NO SELFIES BACK THEN!!

The first Summer back after the Kirkie wilderness nonsense, (I had unfortunately, been made surplus after two years and spent the next two years in Kirkintilloch High School - nice kids, nice staff but not nearly as chaotic as DA- well, on my return Big Peter arranged a school trip.

To Spain.

By bloody bus no less!!

The last person to attempt something that was as stupid and ridiculous as this was probably Cliff Richard.

But it was the early middle 90s and that sort of thing was just the way it was done in those days.

Often nowadays these trips start off with a far more sensible avionic transport arrangement but back then cost was a real consideration, so bus it was.

And by that time I was committed to go.

Now I wouldn't like you to think that Peter arranged the trip in a short period of time over the early summer months or that he had been careless in his planning.

No, demonstrating a high capacity for some sort of OCD behaviour, note then it was just called 'odd' behaviour and note that's not ODD Opposition Defiance Disorder one of those new made-up illnesses, no, Peter's was just regular conventional odd, anyway the big man arranged everything about this trip to the very last detail, i.e. he sorted all monies, activities, documentation etc. Very time consuming but he was outstanding. The whole process had been ongoing for about six months or so.

All the rest of us really had to do was just turn up.

So, the evening of our departure finally arrived, and we boarded the bus.

There was me and Bob at the front on one side of the bus and Peter, sat next to an enormous pile of folders next to us on the other. Also with us were Pat Lat and one of the parents Shona, who sat together.

And there was possibly the best bunch of pupils that were ever put together for any excursion that has ever taken place on the planet. What a brilliant bunch they were.

Our journey to Spain consisted of an overnight drive down to the port. I really can't remember where the port was but assume it was Dover or something similar. Certainly, it was somewhere near the sea!!!

Then there was the ferry across the Channel and the journey through France and into Spain which took us until the following day to get there.

All in all, the journey took in excess of 36 hours. It was serious hard going.

The bus was reasonably comfortable, but it was still a bloody bus after all.

Peter took the opportunity to get all foreign money ready in individual folders with some sort of withdrawal system for each pupil, very time consuming but what a difference it makes to the smooth running of the trip. There was even an individual file for each pupil. I remember thinking Peter should open his own bank.

Of course, then he would be minted. Murray -minted! Hmmm, I'll get my coat.

Back to the journey. Sleeping on the bus was a bit of an art form.
You curl up, you stretch your legs out, you pull them back in, you stick your feet down the aisle, put them on the seat in front, put them over the seat in front or indeed anything at all.

Anything to just allow you to crash out and get a bit of shut eye.

Anyone who has endured that sort of journey themselves will know exactly what I mean. It's torture.

Some of us managed to sleep.

Some of us didn't.

Sadly, Bob was one who definitely didn't.

Well ok, that's not strictly true.

You see just as the bus turned into the long tree lined private access road to the campsite, I noticed Bob quietly dozing off. In a 36 hour journey the Bobster had managed approximately 36 seconds of sleep. Some achievement.

I remember being very wary about shaking him awake!!

And so, we had arrived. I have no idea what the campsite was called or exactly where it was, but I do know that it must have been within an hour or so's drive of Barcelona as that was one of the possible excursions.

It was though, a campsite as I say. Nothing particularly fancy but it worked well. Each of the staff had their own tent which from memory was quite a decent size, I mean, you could actually stand up in it for one thing. It also had an outer part and a bit for you to sleep in.

The kids slept several to a tent and theirs were understandably a bit bigger, but the tents were all grouped together, and I suppose the idea was that we could keep an eye on them. Either that or to protect against a Spanish equivalent of some sort of Cherokee invasion.

Think that was the intention anyway.

Our regular day would basically be of the form: - wake up, shower, breakfast, first activity, lunch, second activity, dinner, free time.

The activities were generally very good, Sailing, canoeing etc., that sort of thing, and in between the activities the campsite 'Ents' people were meant to entertain the kids.

This part wasn't quite so good, so Bob and I took it upon ourselves to organise softball, volleyball, swimming competitions etc. as we felt that Peter had more than done his fair share.

We also took advantage of every spare minute by swimming in the pool between events, so we were really quite bushed by the end of each day.

The girls and Peter would sit in the bar of an evening and watch the football as the World Cup was on somewhere, but Bob and I quite literally crashed out early each evening. It seems incomprehensible to be able to sleep in a hot tent, but it didn't seem to be a problem at all.

Now there was also a very specific routine we adhered to in the morning.

Bob was the one with an alarm.

He would wake up, come to my tent, and wake me up and we would head down to the pool for a few lengths before making our way up to the shower block before the kids used them, i.e. when they were still clean. By the time we were finished we could hit the breakfast bar while the kids were then showering etc. and have a bit of peace to eat.

You get the idea.

But there was one particular day when it didn't go quite so smoothly.

Early morning and there was the usual slap on the top of the tent and Bob shouted me awake.

'I'll get you in the pool' he informed me.

'OK two minutes,' I replied.

So, I got up, stripped off and went to grab my towel and put on my swimming shorts.

Well, you know that way when you just know something's not quite right but you're too groggy to really think it through. Yeah, well after a few seconds it dawned on me as I looked for my shorts that it was far too bright in the tent.

I looked round and to my horror I realised that Bob had not only shouted me awake but had lifted the flap of the tent and thrown it over the top.

There I was standing absolutely bollock naked, effectively exposed to the whole world.

As my eyes adjusted to the light, I looked out the gap and straight in front was one of the girls' tents. I don't know why, but that day they were up already, and their tent door flap was wide open.

And guess what, sitting there right at the entrance to their tent but fortunately with her back to me, was one of the pupils, bikini clad as perhaps she was heading for an early swim too.

Well, there I was effectively standing totally naked right behind her and only a matter of probably about ten feet away.

To this day I have always been very grateful of two things.

Firstly, of course, I am really glad she was facing inward rather than outward of the tent door, and secondly that mobile phones had not been invented at that time and are such a comparatively modern invention.

If they had been then I dread to think what kind of Selfie she might have ended up taking with a naked Dumbarton maths teacher photobombing it. I suspect, in that case, that it could have been a really short career.

Of course, I do totally remember exactly who she was but it's probably not right to say.

After all, her sister is in the police.

18 SPAIN – THE INVASION

Well, as I just described, our days were really tiring to put it mildly. This resulted in me heading to my tent quite early in the evening and entirely beer less.

Except for one night.

There was football on and for whatever reason I had decided to stay up. Really late like ten o'clock or something.

You've got to understand, Bob and I were seriously knackered at the end of each day.

Anyway, we had actually just returned from a quick walk to the local town, and I have no recollection of anything in it at all.

But there were a few bars and us and the kids had a bit of free time to kill, so you get the drift.

Anyone who works with teenagers probably has an idea where this is heading!!

Well back at the bar on the campsite and the first sip just taken when one of the boys burst in.

'There's a crowd of guys running through the campsite with baseball bats and ******** and ***** have just been raped!! ***** has been beaten up too."

In shock I just dived out and ran in the direction he was pointing in without really thinking through the logic of the situation.

It's probably not that common an occurrence, a baseball bat attack on a campsite in a civilised part of Spain. Other clues seemingly confirming the unlikeliness of this event were the absence of said marauding hordes and the actual presence of normal families going about their business.

I got to the back gate of the site where I had been sort of directed, and all suddenly became clear.

The pupils were not meant to have left the site but having emboldened themselves with their purchases from the local town a few of the girls had struck up a 'friendship' with the local lads.

They were a little out of their depth and basically had got a bit of a fright. Not meaning to trivialise it but there was nothing really to it. A few tears and a couple of 'There there's' and all was good.

The local lads at the first site of the tears had scarpered.

Either that or they knew that one day yours truly was going to become a black belt in Tae Kwon Do.

It was probably the first one.

Bob and Peter arrived then and took them all back.

Then I remembered to go looking for *****, who had allegedly been attacked.

He was sitting just outside the campsite round a corner and hidden from view, grinning, and mumbling away quietly and contentedly.

The technical term for his medical state is 'well bevvied,' or it is sometimes referred to as being 'completely off his face,' as, you'll remember, they had been 'sightseeing' unsupervised in the small town and had no doubt taken it upon themselves to immediately seek out as much alcohol as they could possibly consume in as short a period of time as possible.

***** was a brilliant guy and he was in my class and like most of the pupils, we got on really well.

Then a thought occurred to me.

'Hey *****,' I said, 'Is there any chance I can smack you in the mouth?'

'No problem, Mr B' he gracefully replied.

'But wait a minute, you're not a black belt yet are you,' he didn't say.

'No, and indeed I won't have started Taekwondo for another ten years' I didn't reply back to him.

Ok then.

But he did ask me after the conversation that we didn't have, why I wanted to smack him in the mouth.

'Well, it's like this *****. Everyone thinks there's been a mass assault by a crowd of baseball bat wielding thugs'.

'Errrr yes', he replied somewhat nervously.

'Well, if you turn up with a bit of blood dripping from your face it makes the story more authentic and if I sorted it and chased said marauding hordes, think of my reputation. I'll be a hero, a legend, the toast of the Academy'.

Better still, 'Who's NOT going to do homework for me?'

Pause……………………….

'Ah love you Mr B.'

For the record I just walked him back to his tent.

19   SPAIN – SAILING IF YOU'RE A KID DROWNING IF YOU'RE NOT

One of the activities was a thing called Ti-sailing. At least it's called something *like* that anyway and I do apologise as I have utterly no idea how to spell it.

What it involves however, is a small yacht that can hold two people. There is a big sail to catch the wind and after about ten minutes of training, any pair of idiots can sail this thing up and down any waterway.

That is, any pair of idiots except Bob and myself.

All the kids got on fine. No problem at all. No one capsized.

Straight into the boats and up and down the bay the buggers merrily went.

Bob and I cautiously clambered onto ours.

And capsized.

We climbed back in.

And capsized.

We tried it one at a time, and at the same time, we even tried it from the other side.

Nope, every time, yes, we capsized.

I think the Mediterranean must be at least an inch lower due to the amount of seawater we swallowed.

It was truly awful.

It was also utterly ridiculous. We wondered if ours had been waxed or something, or if indeed, we had a broken one.

We just could not get a grip of this vessel.

We took a break and watched as some of the kids did tricks, i.e. some clambered on the front of the boats and applied sun cream standing up whilst their partner nonchalantly steered the craft. Or they stood up and dived into the water, easily getting back on board each time. Up and down, up and down.

Bob and I just sat on the edge of the boat forlornly.

And capsized!!

That trip to Spain was absolutely superb and although very tiring, was one of the best 'holidays' I've ever been on. It was a brilliant crowd of people both staff and pupils and we all got on really well.

The last word on the trip. I was fast asleep one night when suddenly there was a loud bang.

As I came to, I realised it was fireworks and I cursed the noise which had de-slumbered me but immediately what made it even worse was that what must be the biggest sound system on the continent started blasting out Hannah Montana's singer dad redirecting blame about his apparent 'Achy Breaky left and right atria and ventricles'.

I immediately really wished the fireworks would come back instead. I think it was some sort of fiesta.

Waking up I decided to head up to the toilet but there was little light in the campsite, probably the campsite lights were put off so that people could see the fireworks, don't know, but maybe.

Anyway, I tried to edge past one of the tents and as I did, I caught my foot on one of the guy ropes. I tripped into the corner of one of the pupil tents and there was the instantly recognisable but highly suspicious sound of bottles banging together.

I asked myself if this might have been alcohol.

From the tent, 'F*** off that's our carry out ya knob.'

OK - Answer delivered then.

And sure, you know sometimes it's just better not to investigate these things. They were just having fun after all.

And they deserved it. Fantastic pupils. It really was a brilliant, if somewhat exhausting trip.

20 ALTON TOWERS WHERE NOTHING EVER GOES WRONG

Activities week came in round about the time I returned to Dumbarton.
It was the last complete week before the Summer term, Monday to Friday, and consisted of any number of events both inside and outside the school and was the designated time when the various trips abroad were to take place.

It's a bit changed nowadays and has pretty much fallen apart as they try to cram it into the last couple of days of term when most pupils are bunking, and most parents are making the most of the pre-school holiday travel deals.

But back then a whole week of festivities and nonsense took place each year.

There was an individual who went by the name of Mr Kenny Gray, a true legend and loved by absolutely everyone he came into contact with. Kenny was the Head of English, so he was Peter's boss.

He came to see me one day to ask if I'd help him run the Alton Towers trip.

What could be easier I thought, a day on a bus, a trip to the park, then home?

But this was not the case. Oh no no no.

Kenny planned to do an overnighter leaving Monday morning about six and getting to the park about 1pm. We would stay there for the day and then head to a local pizzeria or something similar, then to a local Stoke hotel via some ten-pin bowling before rising at the crack of dawn to get back to the park for another whole day, before leaving the park and heading home, getting back to the school on the second day about 11pm.

He'll never sell this trip out I thought. No chance.

And I was right, of course he didn't.

The bugger sold it out **twice**. We even had a bucketload of reserves.

So we took the decision to run it Monday/Tuesday and repeat the process Thursday/Friday.

However, it was, as you can guess, absolutely brilliant. You see, what you don't know is that Kenny is not human. He is some sort of machine. He is also as mad as a squirrel in a nut factory but seems to be powered by some sort of non-diminishing battery that Elon Musk would kill for. The guy literally just does not stop.

By the time I was flagging on the fourth day he was still as utterly hyper and bonkers as he had been at the start. I'd be trying to grab 40 winks; he would still be trying to convince the kids that the main ingredient in their bottles of coke was the same (di-hydro monoxide he called it) that was the main component of acid rain. The kids didn't have a chemical clue, but they absolutely loved him.

No wonder. I did too. Great guy.

In those days the pupils were really keen to go round the park with us and go on all the same rides as we did. The queues were sometimes ridiculous so of course we liked to wind them up to pass the time.

One of us used to point up at the framework of the roller coaster and we would say things like, 'Unusual arrangement of the wheels there but I'm *sure* it's safe enough,' or 'After that accident last month it's probably safer than ever,' you get the idea. Just enough to cause a bit of panic and doubt.

I used to carry a couple of bolts and pretend to pick them off the ground as the roller coaster cars raced past, really getting the kids going by holding them up in the air and asking things like 'You sure it's ok for these things to come off?'

Well, we always got away with it and over the years the trips to Alton Towers became a bit legendary. It was a brilliant way to get to know the kids really well. My advice to aspiring teachers would be to get involved and give it a go.

Kenny left the school a couple of years later with a well-deserved promotion to the position of Deputy Head in another school and it ended up as my trip to organise. Although it was hard work it was definitely worthwhile.

One year there must have been a spare place or one of the teachers pulled out at the last minute. The world wasn't as politically correct as it is now so Ivana, my wife to be, came with us to help out.

For some reason our trip was a Wednesday/Thursday that year as I had something on at the weekend. Oh, that's right, it was because we were getting married on the Saturday!!
40 hours before getting hitched we were on a bus with 40 or so pupils. Unconventional perhaps, but the best way probably.

Footnote to this tale.

One of the pupils on that trip that day later became my wife's boss. She's now the Director of Education / Attorney General / Imperial Wizard or something for another nearby council, and what an amazing person too. All of us in my family think she's absolutely wonderful.

It is a small world, isn't it?

21 IT GOES HORRIBLY WRONG AT ALTON TOWERS

When I think about Alton Towers it's always sunny and scorching too. It was the nineties, a decade in which it hardly ever seemed to rain. Generally, we didn't take jackets and in the hot weather we cooled off on the log flumes and river rapids type rides.

But it wasn't always sunny.

There was one year we were there, and it was cold. And wet. And windy. More like a regular Scottish summer if we are brutally honest.

Our worthies didn't seem aware of the meteorological difference. They just battered on in tee shirts and shorts regardless.

Now it's worth mentioning that this was a period before mobile phones and the system was basically that if any pupil got into difficulty at all what they had to do was report to any of the kiosks or shops in the site and they would contact the first aid department to come and collect them. I would check in with first aid every hour or so.

So, on the hour I checked in. 'Yes, Dumbarton Academy you say, yes we have *some* pupils from your school, please make your way here asap.'

'*Some,*' I thought. Not 'one', hmmm. This doesn't sound too good.

I made my way back to the first aid station at the front of the park and knocked and went in.

Now there are six beds in the first aid station. Five were occupied.

The rest of the United Kingdom population circa 60 million or so and any foreign visitors had managed to use up a total of ONE bed whereas Dumbarton Academy population around 800 had managed to fill FOUR.

Yes, they're a hard bunch in Dumbarton. A mild hypothermia had set in due to being soaked on river rapids and log flumes. It was as if somehow, they didn't know what wind and rain was.

But there was another occasion which had potentially more serious consequences.

The timeline is quite important for this one.

I got up about 4am to get ready and be at the school for 5.30 am as the bus was leaving at 6am at the latest. Again, this was when I was in charge, so I wanted to be there first.

This time there was a slight change to the format, and we were spending the first day in the Snowdome which is quite near Alton Towers.

All was going fine and dandy until one of the girls crashed into a wall on the ski-slope. We then had to wait a considerable while for her to be treated by the local paramedics and effectively given the all-clear.

So that was fine, but it meant we were running quite late.

The coach took us to our hotel, possibly via food, I can't remember, but when we got there it turns out the hotel was double booked. I have no idea how that can happen or even be allowed to happen, but it did, and I was absolutely raging.

I managed to get hold of the travel company who, in their defence were genuinely very helpful and overall brilliant. You could say they were 'Top Class' to give them a plug. It wasn't their fault they'd been let down, but they were good enough to find us alternative accommodation. Remember, this is all pre mobile phone and internet days so it's not as straightforward as it might be nowadays.

We got to our new hotel, probably around 9pm and we got the kids organised for their rooms. John Christie who was helping me on the trip got me a pint. Just as we sat down to it, the manager came over and asked me to check that the kids were going to the correct rooms as there was ANOTHER school staying there too.

I spent the next hour or two chasing kids from the wrong rooms back to their own rooms. It's amazing how much the pupils in our school seemed to find the OTHER school's pupils so much more attractive and vice versa so it was a while before the respective bunches of over-hormonized pupils were locked down in the correct rooms.

Harmony restored or so I thought, I went back down to the bar. But the rest of the staff had gone to bed by this time.

I made my way to the room I was sharing with John.

On the table between our beds was my pint. Untouched. Just waiting for me.

I reached out and just as I clasped it, there was a knock on the door.

On answering it there were two very distressed pupils.
******'s taken a drug overdose.

Oh Brilliant. (Now after 11pm btw)

Assuming it was nothing and probably a kid being a bit over dramatic I said to John, I'd sort it quickly and headed after them. I got to the room and ****** was sitting sobbing on the end of her bed. I asked her what she had taken, and she said a pack of paracetamols.

I phoned the reception and asked them to call an ambulance.
It arrived (perhaps it was a taxi) and we headed off to the local hospital. I took the opportunity to phone her parents while the doctors gave her a charcoal sandwich or some similar delicacy.

I phoned and told her parents what happened.

'Oh' they said.

And to tell you the truth, that was it. Their response was one of utter disinterest.

It was by now 4am so a full twenty-four hours after waking I was making my way to my own bed at long last.

In the morning I checked at reception for messages from her parents.

There were none. Nothing at all. I've edited my own thoughts about this but yours are probably the same as mine. I actually felt really sorry for the girl.

I did get my own back though. I (accidentally) told them that they had to make an urgent appointment with a gastroenterologist. I just wanted them to make some effort or show some interest. There was no need though. The doctors told me she was fine, but I was really angry, not with her, but with her parents.

The pupils signed a card for me on the bus home. I remember she wrote 'Sorry for being such a nuisance.' She was anything but. I do remember exactly who it was and if she ever gets the chance to read this, please just know you're in the book because you were a terrific kid.

I would recommend Alton Towers trips to any teacher starting out. It's a great place and it's a brilliant way to get to know pupils and what they are genuinely like. The benefits back in the classroom are more than significant and justify the time and effort spent running and organising the event.

Just pace yourself.

22 RANT MODE – IT DOESN'T REALLY HAVE TO MAKE SENSE ANYWAY

Back to stories from the classroom.

As the years went by, I eventually got married. To Ivana. Who I love dearly of course.

However, as any married guy will know, when a woman moves in, certain changes happen in your erstwhile comfortable and organised (i.e. happy) living arrangements. In reality, what happens is, (and I'm sure it's nothing but a complete coincidence) that you totally lose the ability to find anything in your flatted dwelling house that you have seemingly managed to never displace any time, ever before.

8 years and I didn't lose a thing, 8 days (together) and you cannot find squat etc., well anyway I'm sure you get the drift.

For the uninitiated it means that items which have easily been located day after day, week after week, month after month etc. etc. are now no longer so easily found if they are indeed, ever found at all. Things which happily co-existed with you on a shelf, over the back of a chair or in my case 'at the end of the breakfast bar if it didn't have an obvious 'home', all now had a mystical and magical but, surprisingly unbelievably 'difficult to locate,' place where they should be (obviously) kept.

If I use the more honest word 'hidden' you will get a better idea.

This drove me absolutely nuts.

It's God's fault of course.

He took one of Adam's ribs and from it he made Eve.

Sadly, it was the rib that that obviously seemed to know where things are kept!

Well, it just so happened that one day in the classroom some stuff or other couldn't be located. Yes, obviously, and of course I had just misplaced it but as rationality had obviously hurtled out the window that day, I went straight into a serious rant mode.

Even by my standards the rant was a beauty and went something along these lines...

Me: - Where the hell is my (insert whatever item, I had lost, book, bag, notes, pen etc.)? Where I ask you? Where? Where? Where the hell is it?

By the way, I really have no idea what it was, and it probably was something as innocuous as a stapler, nothing major anyway.

Me again: - I definitely put it there. Right there. Right on this very spot. (which was probably inaccurate nonsense)

Me (yet again): I tell you guys; this is what it's like being married and living with a woman!!!!!

Still me (and by now it's developed into more of a soliloquy it seems):- In fact some woman has most definitely been in here. Definitely. She's moved my stuff. Women are always moving stuff. They do it to annoy you. You know that don't you?

And then unfortunately my mouth took over and denied my brain any input into the discussion after that, which as I say, up to now had already only involved myself.

My mouth: Why do you think gay guys are all so bloody happy all the time? Why do you think everything is so bloody 'fabulous' to them? Include in this, of course, the open palmed hand gesture.
It's because they live with bloody men, isn't it? They can find things. They know where their stuff is.   No one hides anything. AArrrggghhh

Pupil: Here Sir. I've just had a thought there.

Me: - What?

Pupil: - Is that why lesbians are all so bloody miserable looking?

Whaaat?

Please note, of course they aren't, and my gay female friends find this hilarious.

23 AIF(HELL)

AIFL - I believe it stands for Assessment is for Learning.

What does that even mean?

The name itself doesn't make much sense.

It's garbage and is promoted by some twat of a professor with a ponytail and an earring. You know the sort. Wrote some books and flogged them to people on the make and to schools who had to be seen to do something about the fall in standards. No concern for the kids at all. It's snake oil. You do things that you know don't work and then you feedback saying how wonderful everything is cause they put you on the spot and you don't want to make a scene in front of your colleagues and more importantly, the boss.

And then everyone bitches about it back in the staffroom!

The crazy thing is the number of schools who have 'Honesty' as one of the words in their mission statements - and what are they all about anyway?

Every school has the same set of words just rearranged into a different order.

Anyway, perhaps they should just have put all the AIFL materials in a combustible **black** box. Just saying!!

But in case you are in any doubt about how pointless these lessons are, the following tale may give you a bit of an insight into their irrelevance.

The pupils were so bored with these pointless activities that they bought anything you told them and believed them to be AIFL educational techniques.

Well again I had another great class so I decided to have a little bit of fun and if that abused the system then that was what would have to be called an added bonus.

Ok, so one year on the last day of March I had a discussion with this class.

I told them that there was just one more AIFL interdisciplinary project for us to do after the previous three but unlike all the other rubbish which took place across the whole school this would only be done in the classroom and the preparation would really just take one day instead of the normal three weeks.

The background to the project was my pretended premise that pupils now in primary schools are so rarely shown numbers before the age of nine that they sometimes get quite frightened of them when they first see them.

Obviously, this is nonsense (ok probably this is nonsense) but by saying it the usual way i.e. with a straight face and nodding whilst putting on a serious look they seemed to buy it.

The thing you have to remember that they were a seriously good, well-mannered, hard-working class.

Never a good idea! – (Joking)

I introduced it by telling them that we were doing the exercise as part of the national project for the IAFD (International Association for Forging Departments) and issued them each with an IAFD number e.g. IAFD 1 / 4 then their individual code.

They signed various disclaimers and documents with personal details making it look very formal as well as guarantees that the council were joint owners of any material that they produced which was subsequently marketed etc.

We then had a brainstorming session for the activities which were to take place the *next morning*.

The basic plan was to try to join up as much work from as many different departments as possible into a quick show in the form of a play, song, poem or dance or anything else they could think of, and we would eventually take the best of this to the primary schools and perform it for their classes.

The next morning the pupils arrived and found that I had removed all the desks and chairs so that we could sit in a circle on the floor like hippies, and feel the love or whatever hippies do, be supportive and all that sort of thing.

Each group got up and performed using a combination of subjects that they had planned the day before and overnight.

It was very impressive and to be honest, fair play to them.

To add credibility, my friend in the current English department, the one and only Miss Caroline O'Brien brought her senior class down to 'help judge them' or something similar. She was complicit in the wind up in other words.

So, we had dancing (PE) combined with singing (Music) whilst reciting prose (English) in French (Modern languages) all the while counting or waving about numbers (the maths bit) that they had coloured in (Art). I think the record was about eleven subjects combined into one act.

At the end all the pupils sat in the circle again and we went through the results, just counting the linked departments and taking loads of notes about how we could adapt and improve. Several 'second goes' took place as there was a genuine desire to help the young and somewhat deprived primary urchins.

So, at the end when we were going through the results and everyone was feeling quite chuffed with their performances, which I must say were genuinely very admirable I took it upon myself to stand up and thank them all. I enquired if they were happy to perform for the primary kids and finally, I asked them if they could remember what IAFD had stood for.

International---Association---for Forging---Departments they recalled.

'Ok,' I said, 'So it couldn't possibly be just because **It's April Fool's Day** (1 / 4)'

There were about three seconds of stunned silence and then with absolutely perfect timing the end of period bell rang.

The class left trying to mouth some reply but were somewhat speechless, while I just smugly lapped it up.

You can file this under Hook Line and Sinker (not for the first time as you'll see later) but it shows that the pupils were being conditioned to buy this rubbish so often they couldn't see how ridiculous it really was.

They sort of got their own back a few lessons later when with impeccable timing an alarm clock rang in my class.

Then another.

Then another until there was an entire cacophony of alarms ringing.

They had all got in early and hidden the clocks throughout the room.

Fair play to them all. Great bunch.

24 SPERM COUNTS

But then once it's fertilised an egg, it gives up, lies back and finally gets to light up a cigarette.

You see that's the difference between 'counts' as a noun and 'counts' as a verb. This is why I like English teachers and indeed P the P (Peter) is the editor in chief of these tales.

However, there is one little story involving sperm counts and, of course, a degree of mischief making on my part.

In one of the classes I had, we had come to the topic of decay functions.

For those who know nothing more about maths than a Covid journalist, a decay function basically starts off quite high and gets lower and lower and closer and closer to zero without touching it. Basically, it looks like a curvy 'L' shape.

That's all the maths you need for this bit.

For whatever convenient reason all the boys were out of the class, so I arranged with the girls to take my lead and go through a particular set of examples when the boys came back.

I have no recollection of what numbers we used but I managed to factor into the calculation something along the lines of the average Dumbarton temperature, the number of hours of sleep and exercise and their age in months.

The numbers were designed in such a way that the people in the examples would be at various stages on the 'Jaffa' scale, (i.e. whether they would be seedless or not) but this being a good class, I knew the boys would test their own spermtastic futures out by putting in their own data.

And obviously they all 'failed'. The numbers had been designed that way.

As the lesson progressed there were a lot of worried looks amongst them, but the embarrassment factor meant no one asked, they just individually checked and double checked the data with increasing concern and panic.

I told them all later that I had made the whole thing up and as ever they were good sports about it.

And I know that I must have been talking 'bollocks.'

How?

Well, as you won't be surprised to hear, I have subsequently taught some of their children!!

25 THE SAGA OF PROFESSOR BON JOVI

Many is a good tale that is 'told' in a pub, but I would like to raise the bar from this and suggest that there are some tales which actually 'start' in a pub that are sometimes even better.

This one is a case in point.

My mates and I spent an obscene amount of time in the pub during the nineties and in one pub in particular. Jinty McGuinty's in Glasgow's West End was the centre of our 1990's universe.

This brilliant watering hole allowed us to be three things: -

1. Drunk.
2. Absolutely hammered drunk.
3. Sometimes very philosophical (argumentative) but also very (hammered) drunk.

Often combinations of the above best sum up our condition.

Well anyway, there was one night for whatever reason we were more number 3 than anything else and the conversation got round to teaching. Whatever the latest gripe or nonsense must have been spoken about and then my good mate Tom slurred the simplest of questions.

"Can I come in and take one of your classes?"

Nowadays you would have to go through a whole load of procedures to find out if you were a child molester, murderer, or anyone of non-woke persuasion but back then no one really cared.

I considered the possible implications carefully, weighing up the pros and cons of this suggestion, considering the benefits and potential harmful and perhaps inappropriate merits of it. I looked at it from all angles.

"No problem" I decided after a couple of seconds.

And that was the start of it. So back up to the bar, no doubt looking sideways and backwards like comedy villains as we went; coming in to do a simple lesson was not going to be good enough for us. Oh no no no no no.

It was going to be and had to be the wind up of all wind ups.

Now if you're ever going to wind a class up of course there's the spontaneous ones and we've discussed the relative merits of untruthfulness earlier on but if you really want to get someone good you have to play a long game.

We did.

Ok so we waited and planned for a couple of months at least.

Now some more background for you to help understand this story.

Tom, who is my best mate, was very good friends with a German girl called Andrea.

She and her pals were air stewardesses for Lufthansa and every couple of months or so they would fly over and have a brilliant time in said watering hole Jinty's.

Although they spoke fluent English and Tom spoke fluent German, I used to carry on saying nonsense German like 'Ich bin keine kugelschreiber,' which translates to I am not a pen. You see, quality stuff. Highbrow wit and all that. However, the German girls all lapped this up. They were all brilliant fun as indeed are all the German people I've ever met.

Significantly, Andrea was also a massive Bon Jovi fan too.

Anyhoo, one night Tom and I had gone out to get a takeaway curry for them and they stayed in my flat while we went along the road to pick it up.

When I got back, they had rerecorded my answering machine message. A talented and tuneful singing one no less.

For younger readers an answering machine was either attached or built into the landline phone and people left vital messages on them for you, usually along the lines of important things like 'Are you in?' etc.

Mobiles destroyed this source of extreme wittery and non-entertainment.

So anyway, back to the story. One Friday which was 24th March 19 ninety something or other, my period 4 class arrived. Once seated I said there was something important that I needed to discuss with them.

'Has anyone here ever heard of the European Union'.

Various nodding took place. They were lying bastards of course.

'Well, we're getting a very special guest next week who's coming to film German Panorama. Any of you watch Panorama?'

Again, for younger readers the BBC used to do investigative journalism and one of the best programmes was Panorama. It's horrible how that programme has become such a shadow of its former self. However, if they ever want to do one on dodgy teaching methods, then perhaps I should give them a call.

Well of course none of them watched it but one question popped up from one of the brighter ones.

'Why are they coming to see us?' she asked.

'It's cause there's a disproportionate number of girls in this class (22 out of 29). One of the highest ratios in Europe!! I actually came up with this on the spot. Years of practice you see. Years of practice.

It was only *one* of the top couple of sets in that year group and the set above actually had a higher ratio, mainly because in about S3/S4 girls are usually better than boys at maths. It's true. Go check it out.

Anyway, I gambled and won, that no one would bother to check this unqualified fact.

'What's his name?'

Bollocks. I had to make something up.

'Professor Bon Jovi' I said.

Stunned silence.

So, remember, one of the secrets of a good lie is pedantic detail. And a lot of nodding.

But for the pedantic detail I said, 'His real name is Professor Bungiove like the singer Jon Bungiove. Thats how you really say and spell it, but it always turns into Bon Jovi.'

'When's he coming?'

'This time next week. Dress smart, you'll be on TV'.

'We don't believe you'.
'Ok, we'll see.'

Well, the next week arrived and fair play to the kids. There was some amount of makeup and hair brushing going on when they lined up outside my room.

And the girls were even worse!!

Tom played his part to a T. He arrived in what I thought was a comedy suit but was actually the suit that he used for interviews, probably now why he's self-employed come to think of it.

He was grinning away (in German) and gave it plenty of Guten Tags etc. as the kids came into the class.

Once settled and final makeups applied Tom handed ME the camera and asked if I 'Vud feelm heem' as he introduced the lesson.

So, let's just think about this for a second. He ACTUALLY asks me to film him. no film crew at all. No one sussed. I ask the kids to look as if they are busy working. All heads go down studiously. Some chin stroking takes place. They look the absolute personification of a hard-working mathematics class.

That's show business, I guess.

So, I'm at the front holding the camcorder. He stands with his back to the class, tilts his head to one side, investigative journalism style, and puts his fingertips together and then says,

'Der Lehrer ist so wunderbar doch im augenblick nicht da. Sprich doch nach dem peep-ton und lasst ne message da.'

This translates approximately to 'The teacher is so wonderful but isn't in at the moment, please leave a message after the tone.' It was the words that Andrea, Sigi and Brigitte had sung as my answer machine message.

'Cool. See that. He's a real German after all' was the only thing I heard whispered.

Well anyway, the lesson took place. We had them doing some ridiculous activities which was all leading to solving a code which was up on the board.

We also had visits from two guests. John Patterson the long-haired hippy teacher who worked next door who Professor Bon Jovi claimed to think was Marti Pellow out of Wet Wet Wet and also the head teacher himself. This was brilliant as it gave our performance serious credibility and actually showed what a great laugh the guy who was head teacher (Mr McKenzie) at the time was. Imagine that scenario in any school now. No chance whatsoever. Poor Headteacher would be toast.

So, by the end of the hour or so we gathered the pupils together. On the board is a code and spaces for a five- and four-letter word.

I asked the professor' So where will you be revealing the answers?'

'On ze raddio vore I theenk.'

'Do any of you listen to radio four?' I kindly translated for the class.

Obviously, none of them did so I asked him if there was anywhere else, he was appearing.

'Ya, on ze raddio vis a tiger, I forget zee name of zis show'.

'Tiger Tim Tiger Tim' yelled the class.

'Ja Ja das ist correct Ja'

'Can we hand in requests?' was the general follow up.

Now let me take you back a bit. Remember the secret to a good wind up is preparation and if possible, play the long game.

We had been in touch with the local radio station where Tiger Tim was a DJ.
And the good Tiger was game.

So, the next morning, the good tiger read out for Donna and Heather and Nicola and Debbie and Laura etc etc, from Professor Bon Jovi and Mr Bhattacharyya…

Yes, hopefully by now you've guessed it.

'April Fool!'

Check the dates. Intro on 24th March, visit on 31st March, Tiger Tim on the radio the day after.

The term for this is 'Done them up like a Kipper!!!

Footnote 1. One of them tried to get me back by getting my car towed away.

Footnote 2. Tom still has that suit.

26 WHEN ALL YOU REALLY NEED IS A MOTORBIKE

There comes a time in a person's life when a man's gotta do what a man's gotta do and so one year during my third spell in Dumbarton I took the plunge and went out and sat my CBT which is the Compulsory Basic Training test for a motorcycle licence.

With as what my darling wife referred to as a midlife crisis in full flow, I then bought myself a motorbike and within what seemed like about three nanoseconds the Yamaha developed a mind of its own, failed to follow my instructions and I immediately fell off!!!

Now, I realise that motorcycle injuries are quite often either very serious or unfortunately sometimes fatal and so I'm not trivialising it.

But this was neither.

I just fell off for no other reason than that I'm a complete knob.

I then sort of rolled and somehow managed to softly smash my shoulder into the kerb. This meant that I ruptured my A/C joint. It's in the shoulder/collar bone area.

It meant that I walked around a bit like that chap in the bell tower of the cathedral in Paris but though it hurt like hell there was no serious damage. Bruised egos do not count of course.

Warning, if this happens to you avoid the German nurse in the Western Fracture clinic.

Her main consideration was to see how hard she could prod my shoulder before I passed out all the time giving me the lecture about why the transplant people call motorbikes 'Ze donor-bikes Ja.' Ha bloody ha.

The Irish doctor the next day was much better, he just wanted to know how easy it was to pass the test as the parking charges in the hospital were ridiculous.

However, as I was put in a sling, I was signed off work for four weeks. (It is the public sector after all) though in saying that I did go back after only three weeks as I detest people who 'play the system'.

So where does this fit in with the daftness of Dumbarton?

Well dear reader, as you will have no doubt have realised by now, I am what is probably known in Roadrunner Coyotesq - Latin as a Lyingus Bastardus.

But, in my defence, with all due respect, the pupils do make it just too damn easy.

So anyway, there was another class I had at this time, and they were, to be completely honest, not amongst the better ones I've ever had, with a few, as senior managers like to call when they want to fob them off on you, 'characters' in the mix. You know the sort, nothing dreadful, just generally not that motivated. And to be honest, it was Foundation maths, so who can blame them?

Well, another of the fundamental rules of teaching is that when you are off work there are various stages in the minds of the pupils that your absence indicates for them. I think it goes something like this: -

1-3 days :- pupils glad of someone else.

4-7 days :- hate new guy, old guy really not bad after all.

8-14 days :- forget the old guy's name, rules, methods, teaching.

14-21 days :- word is, the old teacher must have got the sack   #

21 days plus :- teacher probably died.

My three weeks put me in the sacked/dead zone I assume.

So, on return the conversation goes along these lines.

'What happened to you (Sacked? / Dead? etc)'
'Fell off my motorbike'.

'Oh, that's a terrible shame, we feel your pain, we missed you, and our loss has confirmed our great adoration of you' - I'm sure they would have meant when instead they fell about laughing and called me a twat.

Btw virtually the exact same response I got from my superb colleague and acting head of department Anne Pacher.

Which reminds me I've still to get her back for 'decorating' my bike with L-plates and daisy chains. Maybe she rides a scooter or something!

But let's get back to the class.

Well anyway, then it happened. It just sort of slipped out.

'Guys listen please. But something terrible really did happen.

'What?' one of them mumbled.

Overcome by the level of compassion not heading in my direction I said, 'Because I've got a brain injury.'

I could have added that it also made me start a sentence with a conjunction in my appeal to English teachers to read this opus.

'What does that mean?' they asked.
'Are you some kind of retard now?'

'We don't say retard' I told them, 'They're called new school designers.'
Woops- (again) explanation later.

'Well, what does it mean anyway?'

It means I can remember things from my long-term memory like Pythagoras's theorem for example, but I can't remember any of your names.'

'It's called **C**oncussion **R**elated **A**mnesic **P**erception,' I further elaborated.

Good, eh?

I even wrote it up on the board, but no one picked up on it at all.

And then some more slipped out, and this was the key bit.

'But also………………. I can't remember who I like and dislike!!'

Science should write about this. I knew exactly who I liked and who drove me bonkers but with them not knowing this, they started to play tricks on me, or thought they were anyway. The bad guys became swotty and couldn't do enough to impress. This upset the nice ones who went at it even more to impress and regain their favoured status.

It worked like a treat.

I only had to stop it when they started bringing gifts, but the lasting effect was that the class became a far better group to teach, and it was an all-round better time for us all.

It was also, in many ways, probably one of the best examples I've ever seen of letting bygones be bygones and moving on. This was genuine and was demonstrated by actions rather than the rather contrived 'restorative justice' exercises which teachers get fobbed off with nowadays unfortunately.

So, I thoroughly recommend this 'resetting' technique and it really is good.

But if you want to try it out then perhaps all you need is a motorbike.

\# Not to be sexist but there exists a separate category kept somewhat unfairly for young female teachers.

'Aye, she's definitely up the duff'.

27 DRIVEN UP THE WALLS WITH OCD

Well, I don't know if they all are, but many maths teachers definitely seem inflicted with the condition. My present boss, the sensational Mrs. Pacher that we just met in the last chapter, the jury certainly isn't out on her. Miss a comma, use the wrong font on a spreadsheet and she's rushing off for the antihistamines.

And quite right too. To be honest it's killing me trying to properly punctuate this book properly and not *repeat* unnecessary words!!!

Maths teachers like to be organised. They like to do things in detail. They like accuracy in their measurements. They don't like to listen to other people. They have their own way of doing things.

Ok, so by now you will no doubt realise we are again talking about one maths teacher in particular.

Yes, once again it's another tale involving our Good old Uncle Bob.
And this time it concerns wallpapering.

Bob had instructed Peter and I to be at his house for the purpose of wallpapering one of his rooms on Saturday morning, (ok he just asked nicely if we could help him but that sounds nice and dramatic.)

Prior to this in the school, Bob had all room measurements laid out including space for doors, windows etc. and had calculated exactly how many rolls of paper he would require.
To the dot. Waste not want not. (Remember, we liked our cliches.) He spent ages planning it all out and threatened to do a lesson with his class on 'Area' and perhaps he did, but anyway by the time the day arrived, and we were at his flat to take on the mighty task, Peter and I were under some amount pressure to perform.

Now, normal people put the paper up on the wall and cut off the bits you don't need. That's how you do it. Unfortunately, that's not how Bob does it. He does everything the other way round.

He insisted that each piece was to be cut exactly to size and THEN fitted. So of course, it was a bloody disaster. Every piece took ages, every piece had to be removed several times and rehung (rehanged?). His planning in the school had been a nightmare and after about eight hours of this the three of us had managed to put up a grand total of three pieces. It didn't even cover one wall.

At this stage, even Bob was beginning to see the flaw in his plan but as it was getting late and Peter and I were both too terrified to suggest any change in methodology, Bob decided to call it a day. He very kindly insisted that he would go and get us each a fish supper, so he got changed and headed along the road to the nearest takeaway.

In the half hour or so that he was away, Peter and I put up ALL of the rest of the wallpaper using a somewhat more conventional approach.

Footnote. Bob was very grateful but made us both promise never to tell anyone this story ever.

Oh dear.
Ok everyone, scrub that one.

28 SMOKING IN THE CLASSROOM - IT'S POLITICAL CORRECTNESS GONE MAD

We are always trying to get kids to solve problems in class except of course when we tell them to ignore their problems and hope they'll go away of their own accord.

Maths departments write about the need for 'Problem Solving' in their Departmental Development plans every year then have to ignore it as there is a pretend syllabus and nowadays internally assessed rubbish so no time to detour.

Or more realistically, no time to teach pupils how to actually think!

But maths does have its own share of problem-solving questions even if they are rarely used and with all due respect, it's not a major strength of very many pupils outside of those who appear on those nauseating 'become a teacher' adverts on tv.

'Please sir, I was lying in bed last night and was considering what you said about infinite values. Is it possible that there exists a number greater than infinity?'

Seriously?

What bloody school did advertising executives go to?

The answer is yes. Definitely yes. A number bigger than infinity does exist.

It's the length of the queue of real teachers who want to punch the lights out of the marketing executive who came up with that garbage.

But anyway, one day my class, they were probably in S2 or S3 or thereabouts, were tasked with working out something that was not immediately obvious. In other words, there was some minor piece of thinking required.

Oh, the criminality!

Question asked. No response.

I tried to motivate them.

Questions reformed. Zilch. Nada. Nowt.

'Right guys come on. We can do this, we really can. I know it's not your fault.' (Strategy: deflect blame, release pressure).

Still zilch nada nowt, but now the tiniest flicker of interest.

'How is it not our fault?' one asked.

'It's not your fault, it's the fault of political correctness. That's what's the real culprit.'

Now the mere flicker starts to gently ignite.

'In fact, you know what? It's because they banned smoking in the *classroom*.'

'Whaaat?'

Zilch Nada and Nowt have been relegated to outside the classroom but are still looking in the window and the interest is now smouldering, albeit gently but it's there none the less.

Incredulous yell of 'Seriously. What?'

'What do you mean sir? Could you really smoke in the classroom?'
Pause.

'Of course, you could. Duh!! How do you think we solved problems in Advanced Higher (or Sixth Year Studies) classes in the old days – like a decade ago?

Zilch sticks its head in, and Shock stubs a cigarette out on him.

'How do you think we tackled the major issues of the day, the difficult implicit differentiation, the mind-blowing Maclaurin's theory etc? Eh, how did we do it? Before the internet. Before mobile phones. Well, I'll tell you what we did.'

Dramatic pause.

We lit up.'
'We smoked pipes, didn't we?'

More Pause

Even more pause.

'Oh, did you guys think I meant fags, oh no no no. Don't be ridiculous. We smoked pipes… Ha Ha. Big curly pipes. The girls did too.'

At this stage there was a tad of misbelief gently starting to circulate in the room.

So, for my dramatic scenario not to be stubbed out itself, I elaborated, 'You've all seen pictures of Sherlock Holmes, haven't you? What's he always doing?

Yes, he's always smoking. And what's he smoking? Yes, He's always smoking a big curly pipe. And do you know why? It's because it's scientifically proven to help thinking. The nicotine that's in the tobacco actually stimulates the condorus region of the brain which is actually the problem-solving part.'

'So why did they ban it sir?'

'Health and safety and all that rubbish'

'In my opinion it's political correctness gone mad. The non-smokers used to just sit over at that side of the class, and we used to open the window a little bit. That was it. Nobody minded. We even kept all the pipes up on shelf at the back of the class and took it in turns to bring in the tobacco'.

By this time, I'm wandering around pretending to poke the tobacco into a big curly pipe as the great deerstalker wearing investigator himself did (though I'm not actually sure what poking the tobacco does to a pipe, but I've seen it done in films and things and I think it looks dead cool.)

'That's dead unfair. How are we expected to do this nowadays? Can we not just do that instead. Can we not just smoke? Can we not just open the windows, and someone can keep an edgy?'

'No No No, more than my job's worth.' I said. 'But I've got the next best thing. And it might just work.'

Interest has now booted the rocks of Zilch, Nada and Nowt and the young minds were willing to follow 'Somewhat surprising but makes sense when you think about it' right into battle.

'We can stroke our chins.'

'We what?!!'

The three amigos make a fleeting attempt at a return but are defeated by the command' Try it out. Go on, you'll see.'

So, the class are all sitting there stroking their chins. I slowly meander back over to the board making pipe smoke exhalation noises as I exaggeratedly and repeatedly stroke my chin.

'Let's look at the problem again'.

After about three seconds a dozen hands hit the air.

'Don't stop stroking' I instructed.

The rest of the hands or indeed the hands not holding the invisible pipes of the first responders also hit the air.

Answer given. Problem solved. Much joy.

'Wow, it actually works man. This is brilliant!! I'm going to try it in English.'

You never know. Perhaps there is a kernel of truth in the theory after all.

Footnote: I don't actually smoke.

29 THE ORIGIN OF THE WORD 'DOZEN'

As you will have realised by now, one of my favourite pastimes in the school was lying to children.

There's nothing wrong with it and at least I'm honest enough to admit I did it. In fact, sometimes I just practised lying just for the sake of it. Not for any reasons other than my own personal entertainment. I usually owned up and told them the truth afterwards.

Until the inevitable day that I forgot to.

Picture the scene, the maths lesson is in full flow when suddenly one of the questions in the book uses the word dozen. One of the pupils put his hand up and asked me how many were in a dozen.

'Twelve,' I said, and that would have been the end of it except that the pupil made the fundamental mistake of saying 'Are you sure?'

Well, there was a sparring opportunity if ever I saw one, so I just said 'Of course yes' and mentally stepped back, and to be honest kind of just listened to hear what came out of my mouth next. Even I was quite pleasantly surprised at the outcome.

'Of course, it's twelve. It comes from French chickens.'

There was a bit of a pause / lull / let's wait and see what he says next type of moments.

'You do know that chickens are meant to lay about one egg a day' I said.

Please note that an understanding of the process of egg laying by chickens is a bit of a mystery to most people who don't work on farms. Everyone thinks they know the facts i.e. fertilised / unfertilised / cockerel around / cockerel not around / eggs appear daily / weekly / every so often, but in reality, most people when questioned are just not too sure.

Myself included.

Anyway, let's head back to the story. Here's what my mouth said.

'Well, In France in days gone by, some chickens only laid one egg a month on average and the French thought the chickens were lazy, so these ended up being called Dozy Hens since as you know, Dozy is the French word for lazy.

So of course, we then had 'Le Dozy Hen' which if you say it several times shortens to Le Dozen.

One egg a month from a Dosy Hen meant twelve eggs a year hence a dozen became the name for twelve.'

I was genuinely quite impressed at how I came up with that on the spot.

You see, you've got to practise. It's brilliant fun when you get to master it.

Well anyway, normally what happens is that they say, 'Is that true?' or in their particular vernacular, 'Is it actual?'

But this day my colleague Colin McGugan came to the door just at that exact sodding moment and I got distracted that he was (a) using his legs and not rolling around in his chair (he had a habit of rolling round the class on his swivel chair) and (b) the information he was giving me about the bidding he was doing on eBay at the time.

And then two things happened.

The pupils continued with their work, with most of them accepting but reasonably uninterested in their new knowledge and also my first dose of early Dementia must have set in which resulted in me totally forgetting to tell them I was lying and had made the whole thing up.

Ten seconds, that's all it took. Ten seconds!!

So, what does it matter? To be honest, it doesn't really.

However, I would love to think that somewhere out there one day, one of them by now grown up, believes themselves to be very knowledgeable on the subject and potentially when a dozen gets mentioned in conversation starts to say, 'Listen, fun fact, do you know where the word dozen actually comes from?'

30 PUPIL VOICE

Schools now sometimes like to think that they are businesses. Well sort of. What I really mean by that is that the conventional 'kid goes there to learn from people who know,' sort of attitude is gradually being replaced. In some ways that may even be a good thing but as is often the case with these situations, it often gets taken too far.
We now have committees made up of staff and pupils who ask questions of the 'stakeholders' i.e. the pupils, and feedback their undoubtedly genuine and useful findings to a group of adults who form the basis of the decision-making process.

Sometimes the feedback can be somewhat dubious.

There have been any number of times that pupils have told these committees that they actually want 'more homework, more supported study etc.'

Seriously? It's as if they know for once what answer to give the guy with the clipboard.

My particular favourite was for the Maths dept 'We asked. You told us. We did,' type exercise.
I think it came out of one of these idiotic 'Building the Curriculum' documents that you have to pretend to know about and agree wholeheartedly with at interview (but since I'm not currently pursuing any promotion, I feel I can tell the truth). They are garbage. The puerile ramblings of a fool.

And yes, I can see the obvious hypocrisy with this book. But this is for entertainment remember. They allegedly think what they write matters.

Well, on this exercise the pupils apparently decided they wanted more lunchtime supported study (that they could ignore), more study clubs (that they could choose not to attend) and more time for revision in class, well, ok that one sounds fair.
But with the same number of votes as the first two was the suggestion that I wear a Superman cape. I am sure somewhere this made sense in their minds. However, and for whatever unfathomable reasons I was not aware of, only the first three suggestions made the poster displayed in the corridor.
I remain somewhat suspicious of the methodology.

Could have been worse. Allegedly there is a primary school in Glasgow where the pupils were asked the *two* best things, they were good at. They replied.

We can read.
We can write.
We can count.

That must be where a lot of politicians went as kids!!

But then again, I doctored results for an education course that I was on. I had to. We were tasked with finding 'alternative' methods for teaching. It's that AIFL stuff, you know which is itself an anagram of FAIL. Coincidence, I think not my friends.

Well, passing the course was my only concern so I took on board the suggestion that each member of the class would 'teach' a lesson to the rest. I think they did it in pairs or perhaps groups of three. Can you imagine trying that now? The mental health industry would go, how shall we say it, mental.

Note to self. Find out who sells the 'medicines' and buy lots and lots of shares.

So, each group got up to teach the class. To be honest, fair play to them. They all had a go and made a good effort. It's just that they were all unsurprisingly, rubbish.

Robot voice.

'This is a right-angled triangle.'
'This is the hypotenuse.'
'Find the length of the hypotenuse.'

It's not their fault. They're kids. They did it anyway and in some ways learned a valuable lesson about speaking out in front of their colleagues. As I say, fair play to them.

But in any AIFL activity, 'all the evidence' has to suggest outstanding results so I made up a questionnaire asking how they thought the various lessons had gone. Boxes could simply be ticked on a piece of paper and simple comments added, anonymously of course, and submitted.

78% thought the lessons were outstanding and they learned a lot.
15% thought they were very good with a little bit of room for improvement.
5% thought they were 'so-so' and the remaining 2% didn't think it was very good at all.

Don't get me wrong. That's not what *they* thought. The class all agreed with me that it was rubbish. I just couldn't possibly use their 'pupil voice,' not if I wanted to pass the course.

No, these were just the results, once my mates and I had filled the forms in, one night back in my flat after the pub!!

31 DRESS FOR SUCCESS

When you pass a busy office, you see lots of people dressed really smartly. I worked in the private sector for several years for two pharmaceutical companies and we all wore suits. It was quite strict, so much so, that at one time one of the guys I was on a training course with was told not to come back the next day if he didn't shave. Other organisations either have standards or a uniform but in teaching although the dress codes seem to have vanished it's often quite easy to identify teachers.

Traditionally they are meant to have brown suits and leather patches, but I've never really seen many of these. In olden times some wore capes and indeed when I started one or two of the senior teachers still did. One in particular come to think of it.

Actually, let me digress for a moment here. This guy was called Jim Arnold, a Modern Studies teacher, and he was another brilliant character with bags of personality.

He also had a set of wing mirrors attached to his board so that he could see if pupils were carrying on whilst he was writing on the board.

Imagine how dated that looks now.

Yes, imagine writing on a board!! Scandalous!

But why am I telling you this?

Well, I went through various phases as a young teacher.

Suit - double breasted.

Suit - single breasted (brown and checked I think, bloody hell)

The Bob suit - This was a suit I bought because it was cheap. It was £18.75.

It was referred to as the Bob suit by Peter and myself as I was with Bob when I bought it. I didn't actually want to purchase it, but Bob had insisted that I buy it since:-

'It was a bargain.'

Peter and I learned over the years, you don't argue with Bob.

And a bargain it was indeed, until that is, one day the sunlight shone on it in a particular way through the window of my classroom and I realised the jacket and trousers didn't actually match. Oh well.

Back to fashion, (and how I never quite managed it.)

Braces - Yes, like a nineties yuppie I wore chinos and a pair of braces. Went down quite well to be honest.

Then of course there was my 'Dilligaf' leather jacket. (For those who don't know what 'Dilligaf' stands for, it means 'Do I look Like I Give A F***'

See Kevin Bloody Wilson for details.

And then there was '**The** Jacket'.

This particular jacket had some bizarre elastic which caused it to tighten about halfway down. No idea why I bought it, but I quickly hated it because of the stupid elastic bit. So, I didn't wear it until that is, I got bored and took the elastic out and then it worked perfectly.

And so, I wore it.

And wore it.

And wore it.

Now in the school at the time a brilliant organisation used to come in. They were called LEPRA and raised money to help combat Leprosy. You should look them up, they're seriously good people.

The world could cure that bloody disease for Manchester United's annual spend on overpaid posers by the way. Just putting it out there...

But anyway, shortly after they had visited, a jar suddenly appeared in my class. Just a coffee jar or something. No idea where it came from, or who put it there. These kinds of things just always kept happening to me. Things would randomly appear in my room or on my desk.

I still have a squeaky toy rat from forever ago lying in my desk. Likewise, where from, I do not know. It's just sort of always been there.

Anyway, back to the story and we started filling the jar. After lunch, pupils would pass by and drop spare change into it. So did I, and very quickly the jar started to fill up.

As it was nearing the top and again, this was pre internet and online or even telephone banking I asked the class that I suspected had started it and were generally the main contributors, about how we were going to get this money to the charity.

'What charity?' the class asked in a somewhat confused way.

'The jar. The money in the jar. Is it not for the Lepra charity, all the money?'

Laughter!!!!

Pause.

Confused look on my face, no doubt.

'No (ya knob). It's to get you a new jacket!!

???

My sartorial elegance apparently exists only in my mind unfortunately.

32 NAME AND NUMBER

Ok, so I was bored again.

We had been given some daft training about gender stereotypes and that sort of stuff. You know the sort of thing. All Molly wants is to be an engineer but is told it's a boys' subject. Why can't Peter be a dancer or a nurse?

Come to think of it, the presenters seem to be the only ones who are stuck with stereotypical roles, but they allege this is what the pupils are continuously told.

By whom?

Certainly no one I've ever met.

And even Molly herself, has no recollection of ever being handed this piece of nonsense. But in education, as we know, lack of any evidence doesn't stop an opinion, however daft, becoming an established rule.

So, we were all taken for training where the male teachers were told that even there, we were being sexist for no other reason than we couldn't think of a plausible explanation of why a woman couldn't become an engineer or a scientist. To be honest this really annoyed me.

As any maths teacher will tell you, the girls tend to be far better than the boys in this subject.

So, I decided to do a bit of stirring. You know the like, getting back at the stupidity of the system. I told the class all about our training and they told me they had been given much the same with pretty similar results as the staff. I then told them that we had to stop using their names since if I asked a question and used an expression something like, "What do you think the answer is John?" I would be expecting a 'male' answer whereas "What do you think Julie?" may lead to a somewhat (and much more likely to be correct) female reply.

I don't know what response names like Leslie/Lesley, Jay, Ally/Ali would have been expected to give, but remember this was just my 'fun' nonsense added on to the serious educational drivel so we will probably never find out.

Again, just nod and keep a straight face and kids seem to buy it.

"So, I'm going to give you all your Learning Number" they were informed.

These were issued, basically 10 (Room Ten was my room by this time) 10 (My birthday) and then a random number from 30 to 55 or whatever depending how many were in the class.

All kids were given a card for their desk that I could see as there was no chance of remembering the numbers. A tip is to read these out of a list as if they have been preprinted. Makes it look formal.

And so, it began.

'Excellent answer 10-10-47, I liked how you heard what 10-10=33 said and then did the opposite. What's wrong with you 10-10-54? You stuck?'

'Come on 10-10-38. Quick! Quick! Quick! Be like a duck with a speech impediment.'

'Start writing 10-10-48. Sharp end down.'

It was bonkers, but basically just a bit of a laugh, and the kids bought in to it whether the believed or agreed with it or not. They even renamed their jotters etc.

All was all fine until the next day when the rather flustered, and surprisingly that day, humourless depute came running down to the class saying there had been complaints from one of the mothers about me using numbers instead of their names. So, I related to him the events of the previous day and to be fair to him, he saw the funny intention and laughed. All was good again.

He kind of let the cat out the bag a bit when he followed it up with, 'You know, some parents do moan about absolutely anything. They really do.'

But then confirming the feline's escape, he muttered, 'Typical bloody woman' under his breath as he left the room.

33 STUDENTS – THE GOOD, THE BAD AND THE PRATTS

Let me clarify for you here. You attempt to teach 'pupils.' They're the more often than not shortish ones in front of you waiting with bated breath for your wisdom and knowledge to be imparted uponst them.

Students, however, are the ones who come in from the universities who are learning how to control classes in a real school situation since the universities themselves deal with all the major issues of the day such as gender identification, cultural biases etc. and provide the students with any number of reasons why it would be unfair to ask any pupil to put in a reasonable amount of work and instead to encourage 'effort avoiding' strategies at all times.

Remember, these as we discussed earlier, are called pedagogies.

Honest. It's a real word. I didn't make it up.

Note to self. Stick to task. No ranting.

Anyway, over the years I have encountered and worked with many students. Some have been fantastic, and some have been bloody awful. In recent years I have really tried not to like any students (and often failed miserably) since if you actually start to like them then the only sensible advice you can offer them in all honesty is that they should choose a different career!!

One of the best students that we had in Dumbarton, was an Oxford educated graduate with a PhD who came from Cameroon. Dr Mekwi was his name. He got put in with my S3 class and he gave a lesson about quadratics. I was surprised that there was no response from the class as they were a very keen bunch, but on querying them later they said they had no idea what he was talking about (he did pitch it a bit high to be fair) but that he was soooo nice and it was so interesting listening to him, and they all just enjoyed it so much. He is an absolutely great guy and still a friend but understandably, he moved on to better things.

By the way. He learned from his slight mistake, redid the lesson and everyone totally got it. Top bloke and a really nice guy.

Unfortunately, this tale deals with two of the worst students I have had in class.

We had one guy who came in and was apparently just so damn gifted in that he knew absolutely everything there was to know.

About everything in teaching!

Yes, this expert came in and straightaway told us how we should be doing our jobs. He advised us how we should teach the classes and told me that the bottom class that I had, as he put it *'weren't being pushed enough'* in his opinion. He was incredibly arrogant.

His three weeks watching lessons must have been worth more than the numerous decades of learning we as a department had gone through. But there you go. Some people are just incredibly talented, aren't they?

So, I did what you will be unsurprised to hear. I called his bluff. I got him to teach this bottom class. Or at least try to.

Now when I taught them, they 'only' did about an exercise a period. This was most likely all the work they had done all day across all of their classes, but it was not good enough for our student whose name I can remember but won't reveal.

Just to prove I do remember him, his name began with an R.

Well, arrogant R scoffed at this and made it abundantly clear in the safe haven of the staffroom that he was going to show me how to do the job properly. So, the day and time arrived, and I waited and watched while he attempted to settle the class and when he failed miserably even at this, I stepped in and did it for him.

I then checked my watch and timed him. He banged on for a total of exactly one minute forty-five seconds without any interest or involvement from the pupils themselves, before, with a rather flustered expression, and going quite red, he yelled at them to 'Just get on with your textbook work'.

Positive **R**elationships **A**nd **T**rainee **T**eachers.

But the best and by that, I mean 'best story' goes way back to nineteen ninety something.

I cannot remember the woman's name; I just remember she was a plump woman with a face like a bulldog chewing a wasp.

One day she was in with my 'absolute best class ever' and was taking a lesson. Quite understandably she made a bit of a mistake.

Not in itself a big issue, we all do from time to time, but while the class was working, I quietly, and out of earshot of the kids pointed it out to her and said how she should remedy or improve on it.

Can I emphasise something please?
I was at all times, one hundred per cent courteous and in no way embarrassed or undermined her. The normal response from a civilised human being is usually along the lines of 'Oh thanks, I really appreciate that.'

Now here's the thing.

The courtesy I mentioned only went one way.

She turned straight towards me, got right in my face, and in rather a loud voice (which allowed everyone in the class to hear her ridiculous diatribe) proceeded to inform me that 'When you are teaching the class you CAN do it your way. When I am teaching, I will do it my own (wrong) way.

Now I'm not usually short of a reply as you can tell, but this time she totally caught me off guard.

I've played this back in my mind many times where I sarcastically demand if she knows what a four-sided quadrilateral who's diagonals are equal in length and bisect each other is called, (that's a rectangle by the way) and when she confirms that she does, I tell her to get her fat arse onto the other side of the one which beautifully separates the classroom from the corridor.

But instead of that I just stood there open mouthed, doing some sort of goldfish impression.

But I should have known not to worry.

Thirty pupils immediately came to my rescue.

From that moment on this class (who it has to be said, bring meaning to the word 'class' and who all went on to get higher maths the following year), well they suddenly seemed to lose the ability to remember anything at all about the work or how to answer any question she asked. It was wonderful. I was entirely gobsmacked. They totally blanked her but whenever I interjected or asked a question, they could all suddenly remember everything about everything again. To be honest I found their kind support really quite overwhelming.

Anyway, she took the hint, and we didn't have much communication after that. She just 'observed'. She was a truly shocking individual. Fortunately, in my experience, that type of person is in a minority.

I'm sure she will be running some awful department somewhere nowadays. Nah, probably not, no chance.

As a footnote to this. Round about this time there was a vacancy at our school.

I went to see Arthur and said if they employed her then he could look to replace me too. He burst out laughing and said, "Ain't going to happen my friend. You've just missed Bob and Kathleen. There's nothing to worry about," he said.

"They said the same thing too."

34 SEX AND COMIC BOOK CHARACTERS

I've encountered many people over the years, but one particularly interesting one I'm only going to refer to as Mr T.

He was, when he arrived at Dumbarton, a supply teacher, and a very nice chap, but I couldn't get over how he resembled the Penguin from Batman. I think his overly long cardigan did not help the situation, but as I say he was a nice guy.

Unconventional and a tad eccentric you could also most certainly say about him too.

He had his own way of doing things and I will offer no criticism at all, and I don't want to engender too much compassion for him otherwise, you'll judge me harshly for what I did to him.

Here's exactly what happened.

I went into our maths base one day, and Anne, my boss at the time, and Brian could hardly breathe for laughing. I asked them what was wrong, and Brian told me that Mr T was using my room.

'What's the problem?' I asked, not fully understanding the reasons for her merriment.

'He's teaching sex education in PSE' (personal social education I think it stands for) Anne informed me, doubling up with laughter and spilling her coffee.

'What? Bloody hell. They'll kill him' I gasped as I somewhat heroically ran out of the base towards my room.

By the time I got there, I could hear the raucous laughter and bedlam coming from within.
It was bloody loud. Clapping, shouting, cheering, laughter, much desk slapping, etc.
I opened the door and there was Mr T standing there, extremely red, with one hand stuck in the pocket of his massive cardigan looking for a hanky to mop the copious amounts of sweat pouring down his face. The other hand was wagging a finger and I mean wagging like it had a life of its own, on serious turbo charged autopilot. It didn't stop.

The class quietened as I entered, and I looked around.

Bloody hell. It was all girls. Every single last one of them.

Who would do that to a new young male supply teacher?

The answer to that is Libby, my good friend, the business manager who keeps the school running, sorts everything out, timetables, contracts and in this case, the cover classes, etc and who does a phenomenal job, but who has amongst her many talents, a wicked sense of humour. Oh no, this was no accident!!

He must have really annoyed her, that's all I'm saying.

So, I did the (sort of) right thing. I intervened.

'Well, I'm sure Mr T has told you all about getting pregnant and destroyed the silly myth that you can't get pregnant standing up?', was the first thing I could think of as that tale must have been doing the rounds at the time.

Oh yes, this alerted more than a few.

Mr T then intervened himself.

"We're calling it 'Making babies', Mr B. We are going to call it 'making babies" he said, which I'm sure you'll agree does seem to indicate that he was seemingly missing the entire point of the lesson. All the while as he said this, his finger never stopped going like the clappers.

I looked at him in bewilderment but then turned to the class who were probably quite bewildered too by this point and asked them if he had talked to them about getting pregnant on the pill.

Oh, that certainly shut them up.

Rather suspiciously. Indeed, there were one or two rather worried looking young ladies at that point, but I cast no stone.

Instead, I talked to them about antibiotics and how they can affect birth control and for the next few minutes a decent(ish) lesson took place.

But then, like the scene from I think, Animal House, 'bad' me sort of appeared on my shoulder and took over.

On the desk in front there was a suitcase with a whole load of sex education stuff in it. Condoms, books, diagrams etc.

But best of all there was a big blue erect penis. And testicles too, (attached of course.)

You can maybe see where this is going can't you?

I picked up the genitalia and held it up to look at it.

'What's this, we've got here?' I pretended to enquire.

Actually the outstanding film version of 'The Lord of the Rings' had come out by that time so what I really said was 'What's this, we've got here. My precious!!!'

(Go back and read that bit again and say it like Gollum – My precccciiiioooouuuussss) See, that's much better.

And of course, like Gollum, I did that wavy cradling thing with my fingers for maximum effect.

I then carefully studied it from a variety of angles.

Silence.

I walked towards the door still 'examining' it and then started gently and casually lobbing it between my hands as if testing the weight etc.

And just as I reached the door I turned and said, somewhat philosophically 'Hmm. Oh well. It's a bit on the small side I suppose, but at least it still makes the point.'

I then gently 'tossed' the 'cock and balls' gently over to Mr T who caught them and within seconds he turned very ashen.

And with that, bedlam returned.

Well, after all, if he had annoyed Libby then he was asking for trouble, wasn't he?

35 DRUGS –
THEY REALLY ARE BAD FOR YOUR ARSE

Unfortunately, schools have become dumping grounds for all sorts of useless non-achievers and the council backed underachievers of society.

And if you think I'm referring to pupils, well no, actually, I'm so totally not.

The people I'm referring to, and the ones who are incurring my wrath here are the various assortment of 'youth groups' and assorted 'experts' who come in and tell pupils what basically amounts to what they consider to be an acceptable or indeed the 'correct' way to think.

They will say they are informing them about life issues or perhaps 'raising awareness' of their chosen cause, but of course, they're not.

They fill impressionable minds with all sorts of woke ideas and generally tell them that nothing they do will ever be their fault and then go on to tell them to take no responsibility for their own actions.

The absolute worst of the lot are the drug workers.

I really wonder if they aren't just looking for new customers. They could hardly do a better job of it anyway.

For example, we had one individual who somehow made his way into the school and started off his presentation to the staff on an in-service day by leaving out on each desk a sample of one of a selection of various illegal products (sealed, in his defence) with instructions how to take it 'safely'. and the phenomenal hallucinogenic results that could be expected. They were all colourful and easy to read.
Designed for children you might even say.

They must have paid top dollar to an advertising agency for this. It was a quality display he had put out. It definitely made you want to try some.

Well, we all read all the various pieces of information and then his presentation started. He started talking about issues with drugs that he had seen over the years, sadly not with the carnage it causes to the users and their families but instead to the mind-set of the individual if they are in any way discouraged, disrespected, or criticised at all. His attack was somewhat surprisingly, not directed at the dealers but instead he mainly targeted the teachers and other school staff who are 'judging' pupils and basically not being supportive enough.

The jist of his speech was that it was wrong to condemn drug use just in case any of the pupils had drug users in their family.
I tried to point out to him that this was akin to saying theft wasn't something to be frowned upon in case a pupil's mother liked to stuff a box of Weetabix up her skirt in Asda or something similar.

But this Bollocks Talking Drip Weasel could not see past the cliché of bad teachers condemning poor faultless drug users who obviously were not the real people to blame. (Tories/English/People with trees in their streets etc. being their usual nonsensical targets.)
He wouldn't agree that schools had to be zero tolerance zones.

Anyway, why am I telling you all this?
Well as with everything, the good people of Dumbarton often see things more like I do myself than what officially they are 'thought to think,' by the powers that be.

So, a few days later after the pratt has delivered his promotions to the various year groups, we got to discussing some of the issues back in class.

I always tell the kids that if everyone is putting their own points of view on drugs across then I'd like them to hear mine as well and I then relate the story of attending the funeral of a terrific kid from a different school (Kirkie High) that I worked in who died the first time he took ecstasy. Thankfully, the kids sensibly, were as always, willing to listen to someone not patronising the hell out of them.

But we moved on from that and the discussion became quite animated.

So, to lighten it, I said to the class that despite all the information about side effects, the one thing that seemed to get missed out from ever getting discussed in these situations and that was never considered or mentioned, was that drugs were incredibly bad for your backside.

'Why's that?' the class wanted to know.

'Well, here's the thing,' I said. 'I like you lot. So, if I hear that any of you lot are taking drugs, I'll boot your arse all the way UP the corridor, then turn round and boot it all the way back DOWN.'

Much laughter etc.

It's done deliberately though, only to emphasise my utter contempt for drugs.

But once the laughter had passed, one of the more mouthy ones put up his hand and trying to be cleverer than he actually was, said 'You can't say that. It's illegal to threaten violence on pupils.'

'Oh, can't I', I sarcastically replied.
'Naw ya cannae. I'm reporting you.'
'Well, try telling your folks what I said. See if they complain. Just make sure you spell my name right in the complaint.'

So, at that stage the mood had changed in the class, and it wasn't looking too good and although I had nothing but good intentions, I was a bit wary of how this would pan out in the end.

As always, I should have known better. It's Dumbarton. It's a great place. There was very little to worry about.

So the next day, back in class we had a bit of a follow up discussion, carefully, of course, talking about the previous day. There was the usual 'My folks say this, or My folks say that etc., but the overwhelming consensus was one of definite approval and agreement with the points I had made.'

I decided to see how the land was lying with the original mouthy chap who had complained. He wasn't saying very much at this time and was quieter and more subdued than usual.

'Did you tell your folks what I said?' I asked.
'Uh huh'
'And what happened?'
'They started arguing.'

'Shit', I thought.
'What about?' I said.

'You, and what you said to me,' he replied.

'Ok. I didn't mean any offence. Tell them I'm sorry, it's just that I feel really strongly that these bloody things are incredibly dangerous and I'm worried that the wrong message about safety sometimes gets put across in schools.'

'No, you misunderstand sir. They weren't arguing about what you said. They like what you said. In fact, they like it a lot. And they said you can definitely boot my arse as hard as you like if I ever take drugs'.

'Well, what were they arguing about?' I asked, now somewhat confused.

'They were just arguing about which one of them would get to hold me down when you did it!!'

If one chapter in this tale sums up my relationship with Dumbarton Academy over the years, this is probably the one.

The majority of parents are totally sound and deserve much better from the politicians and the officialdom that they keep getting fobbed off with.

36 (NOT) WORKING THROUGH YOUR LUNCH HOUR

Bollocks to that nonsense!!

Let's just put that out there right away.

Lunch times 'back in the day' were for far more important pastimes.

Football

Five-a-side, Four-a-side, Four v Three, Backie -in Goalies etc.

Our lunch interval in those days was, believe it or not, about an hour long.

There was even an afternoon registration period which only lasted five minutes, but I don't actually recall too many pupils ever being late for it.

That's different now!!

I believe nowadays the lunch interval can be as short as thirty-five minutes in some schools and I strongly suspect the reason for this is based on the proximity of the closest fast-food takeaway in relation to the school.

The idea, which is quite clever really, seems to be that the pupils will not have time to get to said takeaway, and back, before afternoon classes, thereby having to eat whatever healthy delicacy is served up by the canteen.

That said, the delivery service Uber Eats has really screwed with that idea in recent times!!

But back in the day we had about an hour, and we used it wisely. The time breakdown was roughly as follows: -

0-3 minutes: Thrust pupils out of the way to get to staffroom. It was a shootable offence to wait back and help a pupil with some extra problem they may have. Also, if you had kept a kid back to yell at them, you just let them go. Not really sure why the pupils never twigged that period four they could probably get away with murder and no 'end of period' action would ever be taken.

3-5 minutes: Finish sandwich/banana etc., already 80% consumed from morning interval as discussed earlier, as you hurtle down corridor to the PE department.

5-10 minutes: Get changed, get across to games hall, get benches put away, get teams picked.
Game on. We could probably get about half an hour of playing time.

Fifteen minutes before afternoon period: First game over, 'First to two' (new game starting 0-0, first to score two goals wins. Tight games were incredibly problematic of course.

Frantic dash to changing room, pleb level teachers (like me) first into the showers, the almost sub-zero temperature of which even in the height of summer could cause the testicles of a primate made of a copper zinc alloy to become somewhat disconnected.

Important (promoted) teachers who have management time and no registration class, have the luxury of waiting until shower actually heats up of course.
Get changed.

Race across playground and back to classroom.

Try not to sweat too much in front of the pupils!

Yes, this was our lunch activity every day of the week.

I learned this early on in my career. What happened was that in the first month or so of my career at the Academy, Arthur came into my room to see if I was going down to play at lunchtime. I said to him I couldn't as I had a bit of marking to catch up on. The lack of comprehension on Arthur's face was classic. The implied offer was even better. Educational professionalism or football.

Three minutes later I was getting changed.

This took place every single day, well that is except for Fridays when the aforementioned Mr John Christie and myself, would partake in a few alcoholic beverages in the Stags Head pub.

But that's another story.

37 NIGHT BUSES

Every so often a 'sector leading' initiative comes along and instead of trying them out and seeing how they go they get described as I've just said, and the result is usually off the scale bad. Maybe not all as detrimental as group work and endless worksheets whose sole purpose seems to be to prevent pupils from being able to 'think' for themselves, but most are very poor with very few benefits to be had.

One of these dingers back in the day, was the idea that we could have 'adults learning in the class at the same time as pupils. This belter seemed to make no sense at all, except to statisticians charged with keeping people off the unemployment register, but this led to a series of unfortunate events for me.

Anyway, up rocks this woman to the school. She looked a couple of years older than me, had a face like a welder's bench and a grey pallor due to copious amounts of nicotine inhalation and she gets put in my module class. There were only about half a dozen pupils in the class, and all got along really well.
Yet another great bunch.

Bizarrely the tables were set out in groups I confess, and to be honest I have no idea why, since, as you know, I hate groups and avoid them at all costs.

This woman joined the class but instead of joining in with the rest of the pupils, she surprisingly chose to sit away from everyone else, totally unnecessarily, as they were all very welcoming.
She also didn't say much and really only turned up very rarely, mainly in the last couple of days of term.

Ok, so what?

Well, this one night I was 'out and about' in Glasgow and after boozing away with my mates we all headed home and, on this occasion, I decided to get the night bus from George Square with the rest of the guys heading in different directions.

My bus was already there and just as it was about to leave, I staggered on to the bus noticing a group of guys sitting at the back and just as I sat down myself, I clocked this woman-pupil sitting in amongst the group of guys.

But what was much more worrying was that she clocked me as well!!!

My momentum helped me fall into my seat and for the first nanosecond or so, I thought I had got away with it. But oh no.

Nothing is ever that simple, is it?

'Ehhhh, tha's ma mathsss teasher' she shouted loudly and drunkenly from the back of the bus.

I tried to hide.
It didn't work.

'Aawwwrigght surrrr, did I tell ye thas ma mathsss teasher', she reminded the IQ brigade, sitting at the back.

And then she got up. I know this for two reasons.

Firstly, I nervously peaked through the top of the seat and saw her start to stagger over.
The bus hadn't started moving so I tried to get up with a view to cutting my losses and jumping straight off.

But with impeccable timing the bus set off and I fell back into my seat.

She actually very nearly fell too and indeed she did stumble but this almost certainly had more to do with the fact that she was wearing massive high heels and to counter this the most revealing micro mini skirt I've ever seen.

Don't get me wrong, this is normally a good look. Just not this time.

The second reason was that immediately after the group's shouts of Sir Sir etc I heard various of the group demanding a feel of what they were undoubtedly getting an eyeful of from her.

Which was greeted with the response, 'Mibbe efter Ave seen ma mathsssteasher!!'

And so, she staggered towards me and plonked herself down in that 'next to but virtually on top of you' way that drunken people seem to do so well.

'Arrright sir, you're ma mathsss teasher', she helpfully reminded me in case intoxication had made one of us forget.

'Sorry, got to go, I think this is my stop' I said, trying desperately to untangle myself from her.

'But youss jus got oan' she somewhat accurately pointed out.

'I know', I said 'But gotta be somewhere (else)'

'Byeeeee Sir'
And so, I jumped off the bus after one stop. In fact, I don't think it was even a stop. The bus driver just felt sorry for me and let me off at the (red) light.

The last thing I heard as I left the bus at the highest velocity I could muster was 'Thas ma mathsss teasher!!'

And so, I had to make the long walk home.

And then immediately, it started chucking it down.

None of this would have happened of course if they just kept adults out of the bloody classroom.

38 CLASSROOM (IM)POSTERS THEY NEED HANGED SO THEY DO

You see what I did there. The posters would need 'hung' but the people who come up with the posters that adorn every classroom I've ever been in need something done to them, though I admit, capital punishment may be a tad on the excessive side.

That said, they really are rubbish, aren't they?

In a maths class you will be shown what a triangle is, perhaps a circle showing a radius and diameter, undoubtedly a Pythagorean diagram, you get the drift.

They are all awful, designed no doubt, to bore kids senseless, as the tedium stupor helps remove any lingering interest they may have in the subject.

Then there's the motivational posters of course.

Failure is not, 'Not falling down'. Failure is Not getting up.
We welcome mistakes, it's a form of learning.

Really?
What about, 'Before you judge a man, walk a mile in his shoes.'

At least then you can add to it, 'Then at least you are a mile away from him – And of course, you also have his shoes.' I'd like that one up on the wall.

Posters should lead to discussion points.

I had a very philosophical one. It said something along the lines of:-

'Morality is just the self-righteousness of people who have never had to make a dangerous decision.'

It's a good discussion point on the off chance that any kid dares to look at any of the posters in case their eyes burn with the drivel. Maps are great too. You can 'show' them why it would be unreasonable to arrange a coach trip to America.

Yes, of course, it's obviously just too far to drive to!! Duh!

Also, on my wall I had put up an army recruitment poster too as at the time there had been a story in the papers that the teaching unions were against recruitment in schools. Yeah, cause when the country comes under attack, I'm going to feel really safe in the protective hands of the EIS.
In fact, come to think of it, I would probably join the enemy if that was the case. Not the biggest fan. Sorry!

But the big excuse to put drivel on the walls is school values.

What does that even mean?

Respect is always in there. Not regularly demonstrated but it's in there one hundred per cent of the time.

Honesty is another. Why? Did the pupils suspect a dishonest educational establishment?

Is this a secret admission about internal assessment perhaps?

Effort? Nope that one never figures. Not important whether or not people try hard.

Trust? Realistically the same as honesty.

May I 'umbly suggest. **A**mbition, **R**espect, **S**uccess, **E**quity.
But me no buts!!

I took my lead from my good mucker Peter Murray. Every inch of space on the walls of his classroom was covered in something or other. Snippets out of newspapers, bad puns, pictures of him and colleagues from 'back in the day,' and a load of other stuff.

We also had in my room at various times...
Ulrika Johnsson, Posh Spice, Nelson Mandela, Lois Griffin!!

Yes, the star of 'Family Guy' adorned my wall. Pupils used to cringe when I went on about how stunning she was, 'You should see the one where she's in the leather gear' etc.

There was a lot of eye-rolling and head shaking whenever I said this too.

Well, we had a guy in working on supply called Joe, another really nice bloke, who was covering for one of the teachers in the department.

So, Joe and I set up a little wind up on the kids in one of my classes.

Joe brought down to my class some textbooks that he had allegedly borrowed and on entering the class spoke to me about nothing in particular, before 'accidentally' catching site of the said Lois Griffin picture.

He started to get flustered and dropped some of the books and started to blabber about her being his dream woman.

'Have you seen the one where she's in the leather gear?' he asked innocently.

'Oh no not another one, you've got to be kidding, what's wrong with you guys' echoed around the room.

I like to think that the classrooms I created over the years were encouraging of fun and enjoyment. Hopefully they were.

Two other mainstays of the classroom in later years were the picture of the train drawn by Karis my daughter with the train tracks drawn up the way (in the vertical plane I think the term is- it's on the cover anyway).

I used to tell people who saw it that my daughter had drawn it and inevitably they would ask how old she 'IS' Their faces when I said she was a teenager were pictures themselves, so I then let them know that she had drawn it at age three or something.

Another thing we had pinned up for a long time was a rubber glove.

I had a great kid who used to bite her nails. Every time I saw her bite them, I made her wear it. She actually thanked me for it before she left school with her now incredibly perfect fingernails.

You see, it's more than just a maths education that was available in Room 10.

Worth remembering.

One other important item on the walls was a pencil given to me by a wonderful pupil who I am very tempted to name but perhaps shouldn't. We'll refer to her as 'She of great clumsiness and considerable plaster casts,' but nonetheless a phenomenal kid, absolutely superb. She was really badly dyslexic and despite first appearing as unable to do even basic maths, a simple moving of seat and some amount of work on her part meant she ended up easily getting her higher maths. Last I heard she was an accountant. Brilliant person. She wrote a thank you message on the pencil, and I've had it on the wall of my classroom ever since.

I often turned official CfE posters upside down. If you don't know what they are like, there are usually about three billion words written to make it look like a circle. You have to stand three inches away to read it, so no one ever does.

And people actually get paid for coming up with this garbage. Mindfulness is the latest on the hilarity hit parade.

As I said earlier, I liked Peter's room. He actually ran out of space on the walls, so he ended up with posters on the ceiling too. Took ages to read the stuff in his classroom but it was great if you were in on a Please Take.

39 SCHOOL DANCES

Another occasion in the school calendar from yesteryear that is worth a bit of a mention is what was known affectionately in those days as the 'School Dance.'

Nowadays there are a variety of these events, fancy dress, Burn's night, school discos etc but the Christmas school dance always had a certain amount of grandeur attached to it, and it had a style (and mind) of its own.

They were usually split into two individual events with juniors and seniors on successive nights. The junior one took care of itself mainly with rows of young boys on one side of the hall and rows of young girls on the other.
This was further emphasised if there was a ceilidh element to the proceedings where one side could 'pick' a partner from the other side with an unwritten, 'no right to refuse policy'. This was unofficial but heavily and socially enforced during the evening, thus ensuring reasonable levels of participation.

The funny thing about these ceilidhs is that they are all meant to learn a bunch of these crazily named dances, (The dashing white Sergeant - what would it be called nowadays, Ladies and Gentlemen please take a partner for the 'No better than anyone else, multi racial bisexual green campaigner waltz!!) back in their PE lessons but often they did their 'own' dance in their 'own' time.

Nonetheless the occasions seemed to work out quite well.

But the senior dances had an altogether different attraction for many pupils.

It was, of course, an opportunity to get as completely hammered as was humanly possible, on school premises. Mainly, though not entirely, an activity of the pupils rather than the staff.

Two aspects come to mind.

Firstly, in the couple of days leading up to one of the dances back in nineteen ninety-something I had a group of pupils who seemed particularly interested in finding out if I was to be 'working' at the event.

I don't think I was planning to go but after a quite concerted campaign to get my attendance and being asked endlessly by my class to 'not be anti-social' I gave in and said that I would help out.

I'm not quite sure how the next bit happened but a couple of the girls in my 'best class in the world ever,' class suddenly seemed to know what role I would be performing on the night. There were, in terms of the roles for the teachers, the likes of cloakroom attendant, changing room 'guard', tuck shop sales etc but seemingly I was to be placed 'on the door.'

Well, that was to be at the start of the night anyway, when the pupils were due to arrive rather than later on when there is a genuine degree of bouncer work keeping out the banned, the non-attenders and the girl and boyfriends from other schools who try to sneak in.

And why was I to be in that place and at that particular time?

Well, that question was answered when I asked to see the tickets. As the various members of my class and their pals came to sign in, they reached across with a surprisingly energetic smile and wider than usual eyes and for some reason they all reeked……'of extra strong mints.'

Yes, I was on the door, not because they desperately wanted to spend an evening in the company of their 'favourite' teacher, but because they knew there was no way I would 'grass them up' or kick them out.
And some of them were six sheets to the wind.
Hopefully they didn't notice, but you just kept an eye on them to make sure they didn't make complete fools of themselves.

Their plan worked anyway. Of course, I let them all in.

But it must be said, not all of the pupils' plans worked out.

It was common practice for some pupils to stash their carry out in the toilet cisterns during the day and then collect it in the evening thus avoiding being caught sneaking in any alcohol.

And it was also common practice for us to go round and find their booze, which I think John Christie kindly disposed of!!!

I do sometimes wonder if we were sold a dummy and that we only found what we were meant to find, with another secret stash kept somewhere we didn't look.

But there is one other aspect of the dance that is worth a little mention.

As I say, it was a ceilidh, at least in part, so yours truly decided to wear his kilt. I'm not a fan of kilts. I know some people like them, and some people think they look smart.

I don't. I think they look awful, well I certainly do anyway, and I hate wearing one. However, for whatever reason I *was* wearing one that night.

By the way, when I went to get a kilt for my wedding the guy in the shop, obviously trying to ascertain a family tartan asked, 'What name is it?'

'Bhattacharyya.'

'Oooookkkkkk, What about yourself ma'am?' he then asked Ivana.

'Favaretto.'

'Errrrr, then Ok. Eh, any colours you like?'

But I was wearing it all the same that night when two kindly children decided to strike up a conversation.

'Sir. Is that the Bhattacharyya tartan?' one of them asked.

Seriously?

'No, this one is the "Hunting" Bhattacharyya tartan,' I told him.

And in fluent and concise Dumbartonese he first replied 'Actual?' before turning to his mate and said, 'I told you ya dobber!!'

40 THE (DAY AFTER) THE ST.PATRICK'S DAY MASSACRE

March 17th is of course, St. Patrick's Day.

Everyone kids on that they're Irish and basically gets as drunk as possible. This is of course, best suited to the day in question falling on either a Friday or a Saturday as a considerable hangover is almost certainly guaranteed and depending how 'Irish' you have been pretending to be, if you've been indulging in their famous black and white stout, you might not want to put too much distance between your backside and a toilet for a good few hours the next day too.

But sadly, this year the Patron saint of Pissheads was celebrated on a Sunday.

But that wasn't going to stop us. Don't be daft.

We hit the pub in the afternoon, and we drank.

And we cheered the magnificent 'Big George. And we drank.
And we shouted.
And we talked endless and utter nonsense.
And we drank to complete and obscene levels of excess.
And of course, we got utterly spangled.

To be honest, I was completely and utterly out of my face.

And I was still more than half cut the next morning around the middle of period one when I staggered into the school. I wasn't hungover at all; I was just still plastered.

Why was I there, not claiming unforeseen sudden illness or some type of Mental Health Monday Duvet-day. Well, it must be because I'm the consummate professional and I had my (best class in the world ever) class. They may have been doing Higher maths by this time.

Ok, so perhaps a consummate professional who couldn't actually focus on them which became clear as I fell over my desk and collided headfirst with the radiator.

'Who put that there?' I slurred.

I'm sure there was plenty of merriment and laughing (at me) but what happened next was quite outstanding.

I think the Irish girl reminded everyone what day it was yesterday and that this result was exactly what she had expected and predicted all along (from said consummate professional). But then one of them got up and went to leave the class.
I couldn't see who it was, so I said 'Yeah whatssatt half past nine' or some other inane drivel.
But then I noticed another one leave (by the door, not by the window – I'll explain that one for you in a minute #)

'Where you off to?' I enquired during a brief hint of professionalism.
'I'm away to get you a glass of milk to sober you up.'

Then the first one arrived back with a bottle of water for the same reason.
Wow.

Then a third one got up and went to the door. 'I'm away to keep an edgy (lookout) to keep the head teacher away. Can't have you getting sacked.'

It was brilliant, a thing of beauty. Unlike me. These guys actually had my back and sobered me up even though it became crystal clear that there was utterly no chance of any lesson that day.

\# Ok. There was a teacher in the school, nice enough woman, who taught in a different department, but sadly for her, for whatever reason, she really couldn't control her classes. What was happening was that one of the pupils would jump out of the window when she wasn't looking. They would then run round the playground back into her corridor and run down and chap her door before running away. As soon as the poor soul innocently went to answer the door another of the little buggers would jump out the same window and repeat the process. From the kids' point of view the longer they left it the more likely they were to be caught. But the plan was for them all to escape. Anyway, at our departmental meeting rather unprofessionally I felt, this was getting a bit of a discussion. The depute who was in our meeting was asking us what we thought he should do about the situation.
Suggestions included team teaching, having senior management nearby or removing certain pupils.

My solution was simply to put her upstairs.

I actually got grief from the depute for not taking it seriously but as I pointed out to him, it was a great suggestion as any kid with a broken leg is going to take ages to get round to chap her door.

I think he secretly thought it was a great idea.

41 CLASSROOM VISITS AND WHY YOU SHOULD READ YOUR EMAILS

There are various types of classroom visit and they exist for a wide variety of different reasons. Sharing good practice and quality assurance being the two most prominent. In theory they have their uses but more often than not it is quite literally a pointless box ticking exercise where the visitor quietly watches a member of staff 'perform' using materials, resources, and techniques that they would never use under normal circumstances mainly as their years of experience have shown that they don't work.

Today children it's the periodic table – through the medium of dance.

We were even once encouraged to use puppets. I kid you not.

As I described earlier, in the old days, inspectors came in without warning but more recently they only have 'planned' visits which become even more pointless than before because of this.

In my early days my own 'sort of' probation period was signed off with the deputy in the class marking homework. Don't think she looked up once. It suited me anyway so I'm not complaining, and since it was Linda, and since she is a friend, and she gave me a big hug I know it must have been ok.

And anyway, I suspect she knew much more than any visitor.

Anyway, over the years I started to pay scant interest to these visits. To be honest I felt that any member of SMT (Senior Management Team, which later became SLT, Senior Leadership Team, which made a big difference I must say!!!) had the right to come into the class any time they liked, uninvited, as to be honest, they are the ones who ultimately carry the can if things go wrong in a school.

But this led to a rather interesting tale.

One day I had this class who like many I had, were really well behaved for me, but had many 'characters' in it who were regularly kicking off around the school, so I wasn't too surprised when the headteacher, the inimitable Jacqui Lynam came into the class and sat down very close to some of these trouble making pupils.

She was (is) a very good head teacher, very hands on and although she did all the 'talk the talk' daft stuff that she no doubt had to do, she very much delivered the good 'walk the walk' stuff too. I liked her and I think the feeling was mutual, so I had no concerns about her being there. I assumed she was in to check on one of the pupils.

Now the secret of this class was the relationship I had built with them. Some of them had issues, proper ones, and I gave consideration to their needs ignoring some of the stupid advice - fidget spinners, seriously? I also used nicknames and wound them up continuously and they generally seemed to quite like it all.

Well, when the boss is sitting there, I go through my usual repertoire of nonsense, nicknames, wind ups etc including hitting the odd one around the head. The lesson starts and tasks are being done and we were covering work from the board in a quite conventional way, me showing off and generally having a bit of a laugh.

After about fifteen minutes it dawned on me that Jacqui seemed more interested in the lesson than in any of the pupils. I think at one point I may have had my feet up on the desk trying to look relaxed. To be honest I was totally relaxed, all was going swimmingly. But there was just something niggling at the back of my mind that I couldn't quite put my finger on, so I froze the smart board and had a quick, secret, subtle and surreptitious look at the emails, and there it was.

Classroom visit from J Lynam to B Bhattacharyya.

Shit!

There was no lesson plan, no learning intentions, nothing. Just a lesson.

Trying not to panic, I tried to revive the lesson looking for ways of making the lesson look wide awake and interesting all the while trying not to show that I had just found out this was a formal visit.

But, as you probably realise, it didn't work. It's difficult to interrupt a proper lesson and bring in silly voodoo techniques halfway through it, so I just battered on regardless.

At the end of the lesson the kids left, and I waited as a condemned man would for the onslaught.

Surprisingly, there was none. She simply said, 'Great lesson, I enjoyed it' and that was it.

Brilliant, I'd obviously pulled the wool over her eyes and got away with it. I'm a genius, I thought.

Sadly that was NOT the case.

In true Columbo style, just as she reached the door, she turned and said, 'Oh, there's just one more thing. You forgot I was coming today, didn't you?'

Damn. I'm caught.

So as I was caught red handed, all I could do was say, 'Er, I did, yes, and I'm very sorry Jacqui. I *totally* forgot. I really thought I'd got away with it. Tell me, when did you realise?'

'When you froze the board and had a quick, secret, subtle and surreptitious look at your emails ya walloper.'

I added the walloper part in there myself, but it would have been well deserved. Though what she said next was an indication of why she is such a very good head teacher.

She actually said it was better that way as she really saw what went on in classrooms rather than the one of skateboarding teacher using electronic aids (and puppets) for the first time. The staff think they're being clever and are pulling the wool over the Head's eyes, but she said the kids grass the teachers up all the time that they've never seen these resources and that the teacher is 'at it'.

I suppose it's a bit like the idea that the Queen thinks the world smells of paint as every time she visits a place there's some poor guy a hundred yards ahead of her painting everything to make it look fresh.

Yes, Jacqui Lynam was/is one of the very best head teachers I have encountered in my time. She's a true professional.

Unlike me.

42 WHAT HAPPENS TO THE PUPILS WHO CAN'T DO 'ANYTHING?'

That is a question for many years I used to ask myself.

(Hypothetically, of course as I have obviously NEVER met one in Dumbarton!!)

When I say that, I am talking about the ones we sometimes describe as 'Not the sharpest knife in the drawer, Not the brightest bunny in the burrow.' You know the sort. 'The wheel's still spinning but the Hamster's dead.' Those guys.

What on earth did the future hold for these poor souls?

How could they possibly ever gain paid employment?

You did notice I didn't say 'useful' paid employment. Well, due to recent developments I have found that its now quite an easy question to answer.

You see, what they appear to be doing is, they seem to be heavily involved in the design of new schools.

'Oohh, that sounds a bit ranty,' I imagine that you, the reader, must be thinking.

To be honest, it kind of is, but it would certainly explain a thing or two, wouldn't it?

Nowadays it is very common for you to hear politicians of all parties talking about older and existing schools not being 'fit for purpose.'

You and I both know they are lying. How do we know, well, for one reason their lips are moving but also, it's the way it has just become a standard soundbite which they can and never have to justify.

Wow, these people really have turned wasting other people's money into an art form, haven't they?

Incidentally, and surely, it's by pure coincidence the word *'Politics'* seems to be made up from the word *'Poly'* which in Greek means 'many' combined with the word *'ticks.'* These, of course, are just blood sucking leeches.

Just think about that for a minute.

So why do all these new schools get under my skin?

Well, that's because they are rubbish.

We had until 2013 at Dumbarton Academy, a really nice old building.

Yes, it leaked in places and regularly you would see buckets catching rain etc. But the rain was caught and if and when it was necessary, then the roof was fixed.

The classrooms were all well-ventilated. The rooms had plenty of light as well. They all had big chunky radiators which gave off loads of heat and were brilliant for warming your hands or your backside on during the freezing cold winters.

The rooms also all had big boards to write on and specifically the ability to be written on and moved up to allow pupils to refer back to what you were subsequently putting on the boards. In the end they also had the Smart boards put on at the front which can create their own unique problems but more of that, what we shall call 'bare truth' a little later.

Also, the ceilings in all the classrooms were nice and high and so the air was far fresher and there was plenty of space for the teacher and their collection of useful teaching aides also categorised as clutter to be spread around in easy to locate places.

The rooms on the ground floor were also raised up, like upper ground floor flats, so even in your room at lunchtime you didn't have the noses pressed up against the window.

The school had character and I have no doubt whatsoever that this is one of the main reasons the school in those days had such a good vibe going for it.

The new school was an absolute joke despite the fact that stakeholders were no doubt consulted in terms of its design as they are in other new schools.

Stakeholders in terms of new schools include the pupils obviously, the parents to a certain extent, the local authority, no doubt various charities also I believe in certain schools (the bin men?) but there is one group ominously missing from the list of people whose views are taken into account. Yes, that's the plebs at the front of the class each day.

Kind of the main people to decide what is most beneficial if you like, some would say.

In terms of the practicalities inside the classroom, the board was only about three feet wide by about two feet high and only had two panels, thus it was impossible to put more than a tiny amount of work on the board without having to erase it every five minutes leaving nothing for the pupils to refer back to.

As I said, admittedly they did put in Smart boards, and I was considered reasonably unique in using it for anything other than as a screen for PowerPoints or videos, so therefore in practice they could have been made or replaced with a piece of plywood. But where did they then put them?

In the corner, BEHIND the teacher's desk. They were really difficult to see from the front of the other side of the classroom and virtually impossible to see if you weren't in the first couple of rows.

Next to no chance of getting useful information if you sat at the back of the class. Also, as the ceilings were some bizarre floppy tile material, the fixings of the projectors were poorly connected so very often the projector and thus the picture shook as if an earthquake was taking place.

It was really beneficial not to have an overweight member of staff teaching in any of the rooms above you.

The rooms were all supposedly individually climatically controlled but in practice the rooms had two settings, Tropical, i.e. far too hot (especially not great for the many and potentially many more menopausal staff) and Baltic which was fun for the rest of us who weren't of Eskimo persuasion.

Incredibly, the radiators were on the ceiling as if somehow the laws of physics were suspended for these idiot architects.

I think in their defence they followed the mantra that we all run at the pace of our slowest idiot and that they were worried about some moron burning themselves on the radiator if it was positioned on a somewhat dangerous location like say a wall for instance.

But you get the picture. I really didn't like it.

It was definitely not an improvement.

Fortunately, we were spared some of the excesses of the even more modern schools where education takes second billing to sports halls and green virtue signaling, so maybe I should be more grateful that we got off comparatively lightly.

Even the wonderful office staff hated it. (By the way since 1989 EVERY single member of our office staff have been brilliant. FACT, this is so NOT the case elsewhere.) Anyway, instead of having their own room they had some open plan nonsense which looked like some airport but meant in practice they had no privacy for phone calls and were continually disturbed from their work by every wandering pupil in sight.

It was a soulless box but apparently in mitigation it had what were called 'break out areas.' Someone from the council came down on the first day and made a great deal of fuss about these, claiming all sorts of advantages were to be gained but when I asked the SMT what break out areas actually were, none of them seemed to know.

I used to be able to look out of my room and see a castle.

With the new school I could look out and see a wooden hut built over a concrete seat and a flower bed filled with litter.

Sadly, this seems to be the same everywhere. Climatically controlled room temperature effectively just means, as the email I received at Clydebank stated, if it's a little bit warm open one window. If it's really hot, open both. I kid you not. The council sent this email to all staff.

As part of their cost saving initiative, I suggested that they remove the thermostat and replace it with a picture of a thermostat. It would be cheaper and would work just as well as the actual imposter that they had connected to the wall.

And remember I said that the old school leaked from time to time? Well, that's one thing that didn't change. My colleague Anne had a wet patch on her floor apparently from the leaky roof for as long as I can remember, and we were on the GROUND floor.
Upstairs, rooms still got flooded regularly and cracks started appearing on various walls around the school. There are solar panels which are not connected apparently, and cold-water mains taps that run hot. Bit risky drinking that water, I think. In my opinion there is next to zero chance of this building lasting as long as the previous one.

By the way, I really don't want you to think I'm anti-environment or anything like that.

In fact, one time I had a pupil who had been annoying me. When I told him he could get a career in the energy saving industry, he asked, 'How?'

I told him if he lay down in front of my door it would stop the draught coming in.

43 PARENTS EVENINGS

Let's move on to something a bit nicer because the new school as you can tell is a right sore one for me.

Most staff absolutely hated parents' evenings and in the previous few years I have probably started to think of them in similar terms. Not always but sometimes. But, as you probably guess, it wasn't always like this.

When I started out, I used to really like them. To be precise, before the very first parents evening, I definitely did.

I remember being upstairs in the staffroom just before the meeting started, talking to other members of staff saying how much I was looking forward to meeting the parents. They obviously thought I was mad.

For a start the term is Parents 'evening' and as far as I'm concerned that is an after-tea (dinner) event. Evening doesn't start as early as 3pm and in terms of myself attending Parents' evening as a parent in my own kids' school, later on was much better. But I understand it is better for the staff who live far away.

Anyhow regardless, they were often quite interesting affairs. There were in my experience very few 'unsatisfactory' parents, maybe about one per two or three parents' evenings so only about 1 or 2% perhaps.

As I've said earlier the people of Dumbarton just want the best for their children and always treated me with manners and respect.

What was difficult is that there can be as many as about thirty sets of parents waiting to see you and unsurprisingly, they don't all stick to the schedule.

So, what sometimes happens is one gets up, you say your goodbyes and immediately another one slips in who you haven't called from your list.

Ok and that's fair enough, but the problem with this is that although they know who I am and remember there's a name card on my table, quite understandably, I don't necessarily know or remember who they are.

And worse still, they often continue conversations that we may have had perhaps over a year ago, which is very nice and kind and all that, but really quite difficult when you're not sure who you are actually talking to.

But with the glass continuing to be half full here's a few tales.

I have been thanked, criticised, rewarded, fed, offered a hand in marriage (of a daughter by a parent – honestly), hugged, back-slapped, kissed, begged and slagged off at these events, but generally they are a worthwhile and usually quite enjoyable event.

Recently in what is now what I refer to as Session 4 at Dumbarton, they are back to being brilliant again as I must have hit some sort of sweet spot where the parents are very often ex-pupils that I have taught so it feels more like a reunion and has been brilliant fun.

There was one evening many moons ago when I was a bit concerned about my boss, Arthur. I looked up, or rather down the line of tables and saw Arthur with one hand up to the side of his face and looking both rather blank and simultaneously quite worried. I watched him for a while and although he seemed to have plenty of gaps in between parents to see, I wasn't so lucky, so it was quite a while before I got a chance for a quick dash down to his table to see him to see if everything was alright.

I approached him from behind and I tapped him on the shoulder. 'What's wrong? Everything ok?' I tried to enquire.

Arthur jumped and the old-fashioned headphone he had in his ear came flying out. You see, Arthur had been listening to the Rangers game on the radio and the game was obviously very tense at this point.

'It's a penalty to Rangers!' he said.

I went back to my seat and as the night wore on Rangers must have scored, and indeed several more, as by the end of the meeting Arthur was in back slapping mode with any number of parents, who, to be completely honest, were also probably more interested in the score.

I would usually be one of the last out at night, if not the very last, as almost all the parents of the pupils in my classes came in. That's fine. What made it so long was that often parents of pupils NOT in my class sat down and started conversations about siblings who I may have taught, but also for a social catch up. I'm not criticising this by the way, I enjoyed it, and indeed I believe that there should be far more opportunities to talk almost socially to parents. I suspect a lot of informal positives could come out of that.

But one parent who deserves a tale told was the mother of a girl in my Foundation or Access 3 class.

The mother was very nice, and I believe the poor soul actually worked four different jobs so bear that in mind before you think badly of her.

The conversation started with the usual 'So how's she doing?' basic type of opening.

'Well,', I said, 'She's struggling with a lot of the basic work and will need to push herself quite a bit more to get the unit passes.'

'What do you mean 'unit passes?',' she asked.

'Well, there are no external exams in Access 3.'

'Access 3!!' she bellowed, 'Bloody Access 3. That *bitch* told me she was in a Credit class.'

'Er Not yet,' I ventured, 'but if she progresses through this she could do 'Core maths 3 next year and then go on to the Credit equivalent in S6'.

'That bitch, that lying scheming bitch!!!' she hollered. 'She told me she was stressed and worried about whether she would be in the top Higher class and was scared that she might only be in the second one. That bitch, that lying bitch, wait til I get her home. I'm going to kill her.'

Now you will probably have the wrong idea about this lady. She was a good mother; no doubt about that at all, and a lot of the blame has to go to the school at the time, and the information that was given out to parents.

But at least then it may have been accidental and so unintentionally confused parents, nowadays, I suspect the information is deliberately confusing, even I struggle to work out what's what but that's probably intentional since as everyone knows, the standards of education in Scotland have plummeted, so the new grading systems have to allow lies, deceit, and sleight of hand to keep parents in the dark.

And yet think of this, isn't it ironic that all schools have honesty in their so-called values?

One other time deserves mention too.

I started to relate the information to one of the mothers about how terrific her daughter was and how well she was doing in class. Lovely girl. Great attitude, works really well, that sort of thing.

In other words, the usual.

Well, her poor mother does a double take and hits me with, 'Oh you bloody think so, you really bloody think so. Well let me enlighten you Mr Bhattacharyya about that so called 'lovely "bloody" girl' you mention.'

She then goes on to reveal a shocking diatribe of woe about the party (nowadays called a gaff) that her daughter had held in which copious amounts of carnage and damage had been caused to their house.

'If only I'd known, I'd never have left her in the house alone. When I found out about it, I wanted to kill her, then get a good surgeon to bring her back to life, just so I could kill her again.'

She continued, 'I never even had the slightest hint and she never let on,' before finishing with, 'If only I'd known.'
'I'm really sorry to hear that,' I think I mumbled.

But to be honest I was just thanking my lucky stars that I had turned down *my* invitation to the party!!

Yes, even I had bizarrely been invited. Pheww!!

Anyway, I was always grateful to the parents of the pupils at Dumbarton, and it was always nice getting feedback that parents had asked senior managers for me to be their child's teacher.

One final observation.

Pretty much in every meeting the conversation at some point goes along the lines of 'Your son/daughter is a lovely well-behaved child, pleasure to have in the class', you know the sort of thing.

Well, quite often parents would respond along the lines of, 'No, that can't be our kid, surely you must have the wrong child.'

I know it's a modesty and self-deprecation sort of thing, but it always made me laugh and I promised myself that when I was a parent, I wouldn't ever stoop so low as to allow myself to use such a terrible cliche.

That was until the very *first* parent's evening I attended as a parent of my daughter Karis.

Age five in primary one, Mr Nicholson, her then teacher started off with "Well-behaved child, pleasure to have in class,' and I couldn't help myself…

Within a matter of milliseconds, I heard myself saying,

'No, surely you have the wrong child.'

As my good friend Barry says, You can never have too many double standards.

44 IT'S A LONG WAY TO THE TOP

Every morning when the class came in there was a reality battle going on.
Inside my head I was up on stage giving it...

>   Listen I'm here
>   I'll make it quite clear
>   I'm gonna put some boogie in your ear
>   Shake and Bop
>   Don't you stop
>   Dance Like a maniac until you drop

But in reality, it was sadly more like. Good morning class. Come in sit down – Boooooooriiiingg.

Lemmy definitely has the right idea, (Born to Raise Hell) but the message is in many ways the same (if you're willing to stretch the boundaries of reality a little (lot), of course.)

But anyway, I've always been a big fan of music. Problem is I like the same music now as I did forty years ago.
They do say that in the 70's AC/DC were in their 20's and were the greatest band in the world and now, in the 20's, AC/DC are in their 70's and yes, as far as I'm concerned, they are STILL the greatest band in the world.
I concur.

Also, the medium for playing music in the car driving into work in the morning may have changed over the years: - Cassette, CD, I-Pod, Spotify, but the playlist is probably virtually the same as it was when I started.

So where does this fit in with these tales of the classroom?

Well, yours truly was never one to put career progression before fun, nonsense, and enjoyment. I like to think I never 'sold out' etc but I was probably just never that interested if truth be told. And quite possibly just not good enough of course. The interviews are a farce anyway. You score points for getting a 'correct' answer and points are allocated depending how many buzz words you can insert in your answers. Do me a favour.

But I did end up getting roped into an interview for some guidance position.

And so, instead of preparing thoroughly and memorising all the latest catch phrases and nonsense I decided to have my own personal tribute to Brian, Bon, Angus, Cliff, and Malcolm and try to name as many AC/DC songs in my answers.

From the easy ones like, 'When I'm dealing with a *Problem Child* or a pupil who is a real '*Live Wire*' in the class I managed to fit in:

Shot Down in Flames – when a lesson goes wrong

Hell Ain't, a Bad Place to Be – mention of the E-room

Highway to Hell – in terms of trying to keep kids on the road to success.

I was desperate to somehow get in *Dirty Deeds Done Dirt Cheap* but somehow failed. Maybe next time???

Bizarrely, I seem to remember that I actually got the job or a temporary one or something. Interviewer was probably a fan too!

Many years before that I had been interviewed for a job in a different school. Might have been for Assistant Principal teacher in Port Glasgow, just saying. The interview was in the morning, and I was told to phone the school back that afternoon to get the result and so I called them from the only phone available which was the one in the walk-in cupboard just off of Arthur's classroom.

Arthur was sitting at one of the tables in the middle of the class.

I phoned the school (strangely it really was Port Glasgow High School where I would work many years later) and I got put through to the head Teacher after giving my name etc.

He ran through the various good and bad aspects of what we had discussed and told me the result of the interview.

Absolutely ecstatic, I reached out the cupboard door, shouted to get Arthur's attention and gave him a vigorous thumbs up.

With the call over, I put the phone down and went back out, into Arthur's room punching the air.

'Congratulations', says Arthur, looking quite glum. 'I'm delighted for you, that's brilliant. I'm bloody gutted but delighted for you'.

Not really twigging what he meant at first, I said, 'It's brilliant news isn't it. It was a really bloody close thing apparently. I've had quite a narrow escape this time. I nearly got the flaming thing.'

Arthur looked really puzzled so I thought about it for a couple of moments then burst out laughing as I realised his understandable confusion. He had very kindly but mistakenly thought I had got the job. Perhaps he had a more conventional approach to interviews.

(Not absolutely sure he did by the way!!)

I was just relieved that I *didn't* get the job. To be honest, I had utterly no interest in it. You just felt obliged to apply for stuff back then.

No, as I said, I loved Dumbarton and wasn't ready to give up on all the good times for something as ridiculous as career enhancement. That was most certainly not for me.

I loved the rock'n'roll chaos of Dumbarton, the Academy, the department, the town, my mates etc, and so any future planning never really stretched beyond Friday evenings in Jinty McGinty's. It really was that good a place to earn your crust in.

And years later, if asked, I would do *exactly* the same again.

45 SIMMERED PEPPERS AND CHINESE BABIES

Some kids are really gullible but then again so are many adults. Here's another tale which nicely makes the case for proving both.

We had a student teacher in the class. Nice girl doing pretty decent lessons with a reasonably responsive bunch of pupils. All was good in other words.
Well, there was one girl in the class who was absolutely brilliant, not ability wise, but just someone who I hit it off with right from day one. By the time the student was taking them we were covering probability and statistics.

Now, as I say, the lessons from the student were quite sound and all educational goals were most certainly being met but this topic can sometimes be a little bit dry at times.

'Statistically, if I toss (no sniggering at the back) the coin, what's the odds on it landing heads?' and that sort of stuff.

Well after a while, I got quite bored, and interrupting during a pause in the lesson, I said to this girl (the pupil), 'Do you know that statistically one in every five babies born is Chinese?'
'Is it actual?' was the response.

Please note the expression 'Is it actual?' seems to be a Glaswegian expression meaning something like 'Is that really the case?'

'Yes,' I said, 'And do you know what that means for you?'

'No'
'That if you have five children……..one of them is going to be Chinese!!'

And for any Chinese readers then as far as I'm concerned that's a damn good thing too.

But the student didn't get off Scot-free either. She made the mistake of talking about predictions and the opportunity was too good to miss.
'If today is Tuesday we can predict what day tomorrow is,' etc, you know what she was going with.

So, I said, 'Do you know you can predict the future using peppers?'
'Actual?' was the response from the class and the (young) student teacher in unison. 'Actual?' being the abbreviated form of the earlier bastardised vocabulary 'Is it Actual?'

'Yeah. You get some green peppers, some red peppers, a few yellow peppers and ideally one or two orange peppers.'
Pause
'Then you mix them in a frying pan and toss them into the air. Then depending how they land you can predict the future.'

'Can you/Do you actual?' 'Does it work?'

'I don't know; because I don't really believe what I read in the peppers.'

I suspect that non-Glaswegians won't understand this.

46 WHY TRACING PAPER IS SO EXPENSIVE

If you remember earlier, I told you about how in S1 and S2 the pupils used to do a course called SMP and that this course involved a lot of self-teaching. Well, there was also the positive aspect of it that most pupils had a 'job' to do, i.e. something as simple as looking out worksheets, making sure all materials were there in plentiful quantities etc.

I used to try and encourage them to look out for and take care of the resources, as in those days, money was genuinely quite tight unlike now when the government squanders it on nonsense on a daily basis. Yeah, we just 'wasted' our money on textbooks and materials back then.

One thing that for some reason I could never fathom, that seemed to always be in short supply was tracing paper. We were forever running out of the bloody stuff.

Come to think of it, it did look a bit like cigarette roll up papers, didn't it? Maybe there's a connection there. Certainly, as the various smoking bans came in, we seemed to use it less and less and now that the pupils are all vaping (of course they are!!) you hardly ever see it at all. Coincidence? Perhaps, perhaps not.

Well anyway, having tried sarcasm, i.e. 'look after that stuff, it doesn't grow on trees,' with not much luck I went on to create the scenario of why we should look after it and not waste it.

'Why do you always fuss about the tracing paper?' I was asked.

'Because it's so damn expensive' I replied.

Not giving up, the urchin again enquired 'But why? Why do you say that it costs ten times as much as regular paper?'

'And for your information it does grow on trees, all paper does,' another one helpfully added.

'Yeah' I said, but it's so expensive cause it's so hard to find, isn't it?'

'How?' - (NB In Dumbarton the word 'how' often replaces its more appropriate compatriot 'Why').

So, I told him. 'Paper comes from pulped wood as you know'.
I continued, 'And you find normal trees everywhere, don't you?'
'Yeah, but why is that tree so hard to find?'

And then it came to me.

'Well, it's very expensive because as you know the tracing paper tree is almost invisible. That's why we can see through the paper.'

Missing the obvious unlikelihood of a tree with an invisible trunk the young Einstein continued 'But why is it so much more expensive?'

'Well,', I told him. 'It's the cost of all the endless car repairs that adds to the price and makes it so expensive, isn't it?'

'How's that?'

'Well, since you can't see it, you have to just drive around in the forest until you bump into an invisible tree. And of course, that does terrible damage to the front of your car doesn't it.'

And in true Dumbarton style he said, 'Ah yes, of course, that makes sense now.'

47 NEVER LET A KID TELL A JOKE

'Sir, can I tell you a joke?'

Well, that's all the kid said. That's how it began, all sweet and innocent enough.

But I was smart. I knew it could go wrong. So I decided to check whether it was 'safe' if you get my drift.

'Is it racist or sexist? I asked.

'Naw.'

'Is it sectarian or homophobic?'

'Naw man, c'moan. It's just a wee joke.'

'Ok', I said.

His story was this:-

A guy sees a sign advertising a talking dog and it only costs ten pounds. So he goes up to the door, knocks on it and asks about the dog. The owner tells him he's tied up round the back.
So the guy goes round the back, and he sees this old manky dog tied up.
The guy says sarcastically. 'So you must be the talking dog.'
The dog goes' Yeah that's me pal.'

So the guy's a bit shocked and goes 'Whaaaaaaat?'

The dog says 'Let me tell you, my story, buddy. I used to work in airports, security and all that, and I'd hear all the dealers saying who was bringing drugs in. So I'd go straight up and bark at them, but they would just pat me, cause I'm a dead cute dog, and they'd get caught.

But I was that good at it I got called up by the secret service and worked for them for a while, listening in then sneaking up and catching all sorts of spies. To be honest I'm a bit of a hero to the country. I've got medals and all sorts you know.

And I was so good there, they put me in the army and sent me off to Iraq where I'd sneak in behind enemy lines and people would let me, cause no one suspected a dog, then I'd go back and tell our guys the exact coordinates of the enemy and the army would blow them all up'.

So the guy says. 'That's fantastic. That's absolutely brilliant, but why did you stop. Why are you tied up here?'
Dog says,' Oh man, I got caught in a bit of crossfire, took a wee bullet in the hip, right there, see, so I thought, Naw, that's me had enough of this. I'm going home to get married and have some puppies and that's how I've ended up here, but it's a dump this place isn't it?'

The guy says, ' Wow. That's absolutely amazing.

Wait here.'

So he then runs round the front and says to the owner, 'That's the most amazing thing I've ever seen. That dog. He's brilliant. See all the things he's done. I'll buy him. He's fantastic. But tell me, why does he only cost ten pounds?

Now at this stage in the class, all was good.

But then the universe took the opportunity to boot me in the nads and so two things happened pretty much simultaneously.

Firstly, one of the Deputy Head teachers arrived at my door.

And secondly, the pupil with almost perfect timing finished his story by shouting out the punchline across the class:-

Because that wee c**t is a lying ba****d. He never f*****g did any of that sh**e.

Fortunately for all, I think the depute employed a version of that selective hearing loss that they all need to be very good at!!

48 IMELDA

There are many people I have been fortunate to work with over the years but one in particular was an absolutely wonderful woman called Imelda.

Imelda was the lady-janitor for many years in Dumbarton and was simply one of the nicest and finest people I have ever met.

She was kindness personified and quite literally couldn't do enough to help anyone.

When my daughter Karis was about four or five years old, I took her into the school on the last day of term. Imelda took her to the lost property box in the janitor's room and fixed her up with a whole load of abandoned rings and necklaces etc from what must have seemed like an Alladin's cave. Karis loved it.

Imelda could easily have had a career as a professional baker and regularly produced the most wonderful and exquisite home baked delights. I always seemed to find some excuse to be in her room, any time coincidentally, that cake was on the go. Superb stuff.

However, being really nice doesn't get you a free pass from being wound up. So, here's how one of the best ones went.

It all started innocently enough when one day Imelda asked me how I was and as part of the small talk asked if I'd had a nice weekend etc.

'Well, to be honest, not really' I replied. 'To tell you the truth I'm really still raging about the whole thing.'
'Oh dear, why, what's wrong?' she asked with genuine concern.
'Well, you know my flat in Partick?
'Oh yes.'
And you mind I told you about the wee old lady who lives on the top floor?' (Ok, so I had never mentioned any wee old lady mainly because she didn't exist.)
'Yes'

As predicted poor Imelda went into complete 'Oh no something terrible must have happened mode', hands clasped together etc.

'Well remember I said we had some trouble in the close with some kids?'

'Oh no that's right, you did, yes, I remember".

Actually, I hadn't and there wasn't any, but as you are probably starting to realise, if you say it with enough conviction then folk will buy it.

'Well, the wee old lady's flat got broken into'.
'Oh no...'
'Yeah, these wee bastards broke in and raided her house'.
'No! Oh, that's awful.'
'Yeah, and do you know what? They took her husband's medals. The poor wee man died years ago you know. War hero and everything. That's all she had to remember him with.'
'Oh, the absolute bastards' she said, which was the first of only two times that I ever heard her swear.

'Yeah, and you know what's worse? The poor wee woman had a pot of mince on the stove.'
'Oh no, Aw they didn't chuck it about and make a mess or anything did they?'

'Oh, bloody hell no' I said. 'It's much, much worse than that.

They shat in it!'

'They what? Oh my God that's rotten. That's terrible. That's utterly vile, beyond contempt' she said.

'Yeah.' I continued, 'And the real sad bit is that the poor wee soul had just made it for her dinner, and she had to throw half of it away!'

'Oh, the rotters, that's terrible, hanging's too good for these people.' she said, and I shrugged, nodded my sad agreement, and quietly left.

The second time Imelda swore was about an hour later when she walloped me with whatever she was holding at the time when I passed her in the corridor.

'You bastard, what do you mean she had to throw *HALF* of it out.

You absolute rat, you made all that stuff up didn't you!!'

But anyway, my punishment was well worth it. It made me laugh.

And of course, Imelda remains one of my favourite people ever.

Sadly, the cleaners and janitors have not and are not always treated with the respect they deserve, and they are often put in reasonably stressful and often difficult situations with what are admittedly a very small number of abusive pupils.

I insisted, a long time ago, that it was minuted in our departmental meeting that ALL staff should have the same right to be treated equally. It hopefully made a little bit of a difference but that is perhaps for others to judge.

Anyway, Imelda must have approved or at least forgiven me for my badness because when she retired from the school, she left a card for me thanking me for, in her words, supporting her more than anyone else did.

To be honest. I was very proud of that honour as Imelda is yet another of the many phenomenal people, I have had the privilege to work with over the years.

49 ACTIVITIES WEEK – JOHNSTON STYLE

As we've discussed earlier Dumbarton Academy used to run a pretty successful week of different activities for the pupils each year in the last full week before the summer.

Well, during my repping time, I took a trip down to Dumbarton to see all my, at that time, ex-colleagues. My plan was to go in and look around to see who was there and to call on the likes of Peter and Bob and shoot the breeze for a while.
As a rep we would call it recharging the batteries or 'planning', but it was really just me skiving for a while.

Anyway, as I approached the school heading down Crosslet Road, I had to pass the old games hall which was a separate block from the main building which looked like an old if somewhat lowish aircraft hangar and then passed the school gymnasium which was connected to the main building of the school. Between these two buildings was a patch of grass and on the day that I visited, there was Bob Johnston lying out sunbathing on the closest thing he could find to a deck chair.

He was not too busy in other words.

So, we chatted for a bit and Bob informed me of what he had done the previous day and indeed all other days that week.

The order of business went something along these lines.

Bob signs up to run a 'gym' for pupils.

Bob arrives at the school gymnasium and unlocks the padlock to open the cupboard door to get to the weights.
He brings all weights out and sets up dumbbells and barbells etc.
In the absence of any kids Bob does a forty-five-minute workout.
Bob puts weights etc back in the cupboard and goes to shower and get changed.

And this is the good bit.
He then gets into his car and leaves to go to his golf course which from memory was on the other side of Paisley and plays nine holes or so.
Bob then drives back to the school and repeats the entire weights process.

And all this with not a kid or another member of staff ever daring to annoy or bother him.

He managed to repeat this every day for the full week Monday to Friday.

Somehow or other he even managed to get the sun to shine. And yes, that's the bit that is probably the hardest to believe. It was actually sunny for five successive days that year.

Must have been the 90s.

I've got my own version of a relaxing activities week now as well I need to add. Brian and I take a bunch of kids out to play football.

How is it so relaxing for me?

Well, I just pass the ball to Brian, and I could literally get changed and go for a game of golf and come back and rejoin the game, and none of the kids would have been able to get the ball off Brian. He is *utterly* outstanding – and he's a brilliant player too!!!

50 THE OTHER DEPARTMENTS

As you will undoubtedly know, secondary schools are made up of a variety of departments who all play their own particular roles in creating these 'well rounded' pupils we seem to have nowadays.

Over the years there has been a bit of a move towards some kind of generic teaching, a bit like as if secondary school was really primary 8 to 13 or so. I think that sadly, there are many people who would like this to be the case.

I place myself firmly in the opposite camp. I think we are all different and that's a good thing.

In life many things are different and it's a bit of a con to try to make young people think otherwise. The other main reason I don't like it, is that it is taking away many of the genuine subject enthusiasts and bizarre characters who used to populate schools and infuse their eccentricities upon the pupils.

In the past, the language departments which now go under the generic heading of 'Modern Languages' which always makes me wonder what they think these guys in the past used to teach Aramaic, Babylonian? Well, back then they were given the far more informative names French, German, Spanish etc. These departments always seemed to have someone known as Madame something or other. Of course, then it was mainly a woman who took on this role!! Ha ha. It sort of set a tone.

I think they should bring that back.

The modern languages people now are all really nice, and do a brilliant job, but it is just not quite the same. In their defence it's probably a lot more sane than it was back in the past.

Science guys in their mind seemed to think back then, that they were one phone call from being consulted by NASA or in the case of Biology and Chemistry perhaps Dr Frankenstein might have been more appropriate caller. Commitment to the cause by these guys is not questioned by myself at all, but it was sometimes off the scale when I started teaching.

There was one Chemistry teacher, the inimitable Doc Gorton who managed to genuinely blow up a lab during a lesson and according to rumour, whilst still smouldering from the explosion, and with parts of the room still on fire continued his lesson completely unphased to a class of bemused, engrossed and no doubt slightly terrified pupils.

PE back in the day, was just the physical side, no writing but it gave licence for PE teachers to really boot arses and more people seemed to enjoy it then. They have now had to shoehorn in a whole load of essays and things, and I think a lot of pupils get put off by this.

My good friend John Hammond, who by the way, is one of the hardest working individuals ever, says he actually had to get one group of pupils (the boys) to go easy on the other group (the girls) in a physical assessment. He knew it was daft, but he just had to go along with it. PE is a subject I think I would like to have taught. Well with the exception of the social dancing. That would be a nightmare, as would working with Debs or Steph if you had a hangover. These guys (who I love, and think are fantastic) really just have too much energy. Wonder what would happen if they went on a trip with Kenny Gray. Hmmm.

One thing that hasn't changed throughout my career is that my favourite other department in the school has always been the English department. It is a great subject and vital in terms of teaching how to express yourself or how to interpret some information but the one part I can never get my head around is the 'hidden meanings.'

By that I mean when they ask things like for example, 'What does the author mean when she mentions a lighthouse? What is she trying to get the lighthouse to signify?

My answer would no doubt include some reference to a justifiable concern about rocks at the foot of a cliff or the like, but inevitably it would turn out that said author was really trying to relay his or her worldly view of religion.

To be honest I'm really just not clever enough to get it.

However, more power to English teachers.

At any stage in my career my favourites have always been in that department. From Peter and Kenny with Awdrey, Ann, Jo, Pat, Cathy and Sheila (she of petite stature and enormous staffroom chair), when I started right up to now with the likes of Ashliegh (spelled right) who I could listen to all day, she's wonderful, she should make relaxation tapes or something, to my most recent favourite, the one and only Miss Caroline O'Brien.

For a newish younger teacher, (well she's a lot newer and younger than me) my goodness she is certainly 'old school' in terms of being a character.
Literally every pupil loves her, and she rips it right out of them all. Sometimes even worse than I do. But at the same time, she manages to have total respect like no one else I know.

I tell the pupils that sometimes she gets a bit tired because she works part time for GCHQ using all that hidden meaning training, intercepting, and then decoding spy messages from enemies of the UK. The Great Gatsby is the code book that she uses and that's why they have to read it, even though it's so bad. (apologies to English dept – I know you all love it.)

The kids buy into this every time but come to think of it for all I know, perhaps she does work for GCHQ.

But as I was saying, there is more of a move to the idea that we all 'teach children' nowadays. It is yet another non improvement in the system but let's hope it returns to the previous way. If you enjoy your subject, you will be more motivated I believe, and enjoy the job more.

The subjects are all different. They are all hard in their own way. Everyone thinks their own subject is the hardest to teach. Maths teachers are of course the ones who are correct in this assumption. The rest are wrong.

My book, my opinions. So there!!

But in saying that, there are so many great subjects and great people out there that the whole of the pupil is greater than the sum of its parts. Or something like that anyway.

I seem to be struggling to communicate this last idea across here.
Perhaps I need the services of an English teacher.

Anyone know a good one?

51 SMART BOARDS – THE NAKED TRUTH

About half a dozen or so years into the twenty first century someone up at the National Education Department or whatever it's called, (which I've just realised it probably can't be as that has the initials NED - surely just a coincidence, c'mon!!), well they decided that pupil education would be enhanced if the wipeable whiteboard which had itself replaced the chalk blackboard could *itself* be replaced by the 'interactive' whiteboard.

Whilst I now really like them and use them all the time, there is still a very small part of me that sometimes thinks that maybe, just maybe it's not so much a screen as instead some sort of camera or two-way mirror and that on the other side are a group of psychiatric doctors watching me, the mental patient, living in his own fantasy (school) world: -

"Observe, Nurse, how the patient speaks to himself as if there are a number of young people inside the cell with him.'

"Yes Doctor, he really does seem to believe that he actually is some kind of a teacher in a classroom or something."

"Let's up his dosage and see if we can find out more about those other 'friends' he talks about, what were they called?"

Nurse consults notes.

"He seems to talk a lot about someone called Bob. Then there's a Peter, a John, and an Arthur mainly, but believe it or not, he created some Home Economics teacher yesterday called, would you believe it? A Carol COOK!! He's really not very creative, is he?"

"He's beyond help you know. Even claims to know some sort of distance runner named Murray or sometimes calls him Hanvey or something, says the poor chap just chases kids round the 'school' all day – as if that would ever happen!!"

"Think it's Maths the patient pretends to teach – It really makes no sense, all gibberish. He's a hopeless case anyway".

"Have you noticed that every time we get the cattle prod out a fellow called (consults notes again) 'Westy' appears shouting Here! Here!"

"The cattle prod must be why this 'Westy' chap walks like that.

"Oh, here, you seem to have fallen off your stool laughing, let me help you".

I can never 'quite' get that thought out of my mind entirely!!

Anyway, back then, (at the introduction of Smart boards) the warning signs were there.

There was unofficial information and rumours circulating that the younger primary kids 'loved' these things which is usually a good indication that nothing of educational or intellectual substance ever took place on them.

I'm sorry, a kid slapping a number 8 when two fours light up is hardly sector leading and realistically teaches them very little but officially these boards were going to help stop the worryingly ongoing decline of Scottish Education.

One thing that was allowed to slip by was the fact that the projectors had bulbs which cost the council in excess of £300 each.

Maths not being their strong point, I often wondered why the same projectors (not just the bloody bulbs) could be bought for much less than this, but no doubt someone was at it somewhere.

Anyway, the boards and projectors were fitted to every class.

We had our concerns and so for some reason, bets were hedged, and the boards were fitted at the side of the class rather than at the front which would probably have made more sense. The original boards were left in place at the front.

The significance of this minor detail will be revealed shortly.

Well as you can imagine, we were under pressure to use these things but there were very few resources back then and it took a great deal of time at first to learn HOW to use them and then to learn how to write on them and for your writing not to look as if you were suffering from some sort of a seizure during the process.

So, what happened was that many teachers 'enhanced' their lessons with reasonably pointless videos, i.e. there was no interaction at all, teachers just using the projector as errr hmmm, a projector and the £3000 (thousand, yes) Smart board like a £20 plywood screen instead.

As did we.

Now as I've said, it was on the side of my room, on the side opposite the windows. If you can visualise the set-up, imagine you have your back to the window (and there are no curtains on this south facing room). This is where I stood a lot of the time, sort of in the area of the corner between the window side and the front of the classroom which would be on your left.

The pupils would be pretty much on your right and facing the front and using the original board also on my left but straight in front of them.

To view the Smart board, the pupils had to turn to the right. I always liked this seating arrangement; group work should be banned in my opinion. It just stops pupils having to think for themselves, but sadly perhaps that is the cunning plan.

Anyway, if you've got your bearings then visualise me standing there. If you've done it right, then you will realise that I am actually the only one with the Smart board in my line of sight.

This is the important bit to remember!

So, some lesson was taking place and the lesson had been suitably 'enhanced' with some little video snippet at some point and was now safely being ignored while the pupils worked through the proper lesson in front of them.

But I didn't feel any reason to turn the Smart board off.

It was just left on in the background. (or rather the sideground, is that a word?)

Firstly, let me say that whatever site it was on, was a legitimate West Dunbartonshire Council approved website so that's my defence sorted. There was the main window on the screen and a few smaller windows surrounding it advertising pens, books, videos, and other such rubbish.

But several minutes into the lesson things changed.

In my peripheral vision I noticed that the advert on the bottom right changed suddenly.

Not so much an advert anymore. More like, the sort of activity that takes place just after the well-endowed plumber gets called round to fix the stunning and surprisingly clothes free, yet very attractive housewife's washing machine etc.

Yes, yours truly had somehow managed to show a porno in the class. I had apparently, incorrectly assumed and thought that there were meant to be restrictions and things to block this out from schools.
This is why I went into detail of who was sitting where and line of sight etc.

Because you see, no one at all saw it.

Not one pupil had actually looked round.
They were all either working or looking at the board in front of them. Fortunately for me, the board must have been on some sort of silent setting.

However, what the pupils did properly see was me suited and booted, quite literally dive across the classroom, then slide across the desk knocking an assortment of jotters, pens, rulers, books etc out of the way and finally reach out, grab and pull the extension socket plug right out of the wall.

I lay there sprawled and crumpled on the floor, half under the computer table, plug socket in hand.

And yet absolutely no one seemed remotely surprised or concerned!! Again, no one batted an eye.

By the way, as an aside, nowadays it would probably be reasonably safe if something like this happened again in most of the classrooms, as the kids are generally discouraged from looking at the boards anymore.

And anyway, they are probably all glued to their bloody phones.

'I Think the bulb was about to overheat,' I tried to say as a way of explanation, as I crawled back up into some sort of seating or standing position.

'Makes sense', I heard one guy in the middle of the class say to everyone.

'My dad says the bulbs cost in excess of £300 each.'

52 FIRE PREVENTION

Some people smoke. If you exclude the Sherlock Holmes inspired pipe/thinking situation we discussed earlier, then I don't smoke.

I never have and, in the past, it used to really annoy me. Not so much now and to be honest it's now ironically got to the point that I have quite a lot of sympathy for the few remaining nicotine ninjas who sadly get treated like lepers nowadays.

But though I have mellowed over the years my good buddy Bob most certainly has not.
All smokers would be hung drawn and quartered if it was up to him. He really does despise the habit.

And as you know he is a law unto himself of course.

So where are we going with this?

Well, at the end of the maths corridor on the ground floor was Bob's room. It became mine when he retired but at the time as you may remember, I was in the one next door.
Next to Bob's room on the other side, there was nothing except playground.

Conveniently positioned out of line of sight of any classrooms or deputy head teacher's offices.

So, of course, that ironically made it ideal nicotine inhalation territory.

Now, I didn't see any of this actually happen but I have it on very good authority that it was a genuine event so I will try to relay the events as best and as accurately as I can.

Ok, so Bob was standing in the corridor outside his classroom, locking up before going upstairs to the staffroom.

Well, he wouldn't have been properly locking up as no one would have ever dared go into his class and come to think of it no one robbed anything back then. But suffice to say, for whatever reason, he was in the corridor anyway.

When he saw smoke.

Just outside the window at the end of the corridor, wafting gently upwards into the sky.

Now he could of course, simply have gone outside and yelled at them if he thought there were smokers having the audacity to pollute the air which then lingered on or near the outside of his classroom.

If he genuinely thought, there was a fire or the risk of a fire he could have picked up the fire extinguisher or perhaps rung the alarm.

No, of course that didn't happen.

The great one took decisive action, and as usual did it with a flourish and in his own unique style.

First, he fixed his tie and jacket, then marched up to the staffroom where he filled the kettle with water.

He then proceeded to stride back down to his room, well actually the window outside his room at the end of the corridor, opened the window and poured the contents of the kettle over whatever 'highly dangerous combustible material' there must have been out there.

You can now add voluntary fire fighter to the cv of this heroic individual.

And yet again - no one said a thing.

Even the daft, and by this time, utterly drenched smokers didn't complain. I suspect they were just probably glad that Bob had somewhat fortuitously forgotten to boil the water first.

Footnote. I have made the assumption that it was only pupils who were outside smoking. Of course, that is not necessarily the case.

53 MARY (MARY)

Do you see what I did there? That's no accident. Chapter 53 is dedicated to Mary Gallagher, one of my favourite learning assistants of all time and her nickname which as we will soon learn was Mary 'Two-Times'.

Mary was a great wee woman who was one of these people with a heart of gold who just really liked helping people. I think she did work for her church, or a charity and I know from time to time she would collect money or keep stuff you were throwing out.

But she had a terrible habit of repeating the last couple of words you said.

'It's bloody roasting in here.'
'...in here' she'd reply.

'Need to get more textbooks and jotters'.
'...textbooks and jotters' etc etc.

You get the idea.

'He's a smart guy, she's a hard worker but he's a little bastard'.
'...little bastard'.

It was always a game with my colleague Brian to try to get her to say something ridiculous or better still to swear like a trooper and it provided us with great entertainment.

It was all done in fun, and I had the highest regard for her. During a difficult time in the school under the reign of one particular head teacher we were all under the cosh as he was definitely trying to 'get us.' Having Mary in the class as a witness at the time, was brilliant (and she hated him) and for that, I always appreciated the help and support she offered.

But there's another aspect to Mary that you might find interesting.

Another learning assistant was in the class with me one day. About ten minutes before the end of the period I said to her it was ok if she wanted to leave early to 'get her paperwork done.'

She looked at me quite puzzled.

'What paperwork?' she asked.
'You know the stuff you have to write up at the end of each period,' I tried to advise her helpfully.

'Again, sorry what paperwork?' she repeated, now starting to sound just a little bit worried in case she had suddenly and inadvertently found out that she wasn't doing her job properly.

'I don't know,' I said. 'Mary leaves ten minutes early each day to get hers done.'

The other learning assistant then burst out laughing.
'Paperwork? Ha Ha! Brilliant. That's just what she calls rolling up her cigarettes.'

You see, every period bloody Mary had fleeced me. Got to leave ten minutes early for a smoke. Outstanding. What a woman.

As I say, she is a terrific individual, and another one that I really liked.

Though for some reason that I can't quite put my finger on, and I know I'm going out on a limb here, I really don't think that her and Bob would have hit it off!!

54 THE CRIT

I'm very fortunate in that I have always found most pupils in any class to be reasonably nice and kinder and more considerate than not.

There are only one or two occasions when I can think of it being different to this, and neither of these times were actually in Dumbarton.

But I feel pupils have generally 'had my back' so to speak over the years and this goes right back to when I was a student on placement at Bearsden Academy.

Ok, so I had this 'dodgy' class in either S1 or S2, I can't remember which, but they were working through the individualised SMP course at the time.

I had my 'crit' with this class and for those outside the profession, a crit is the sort of equivalence of a driving test, that is, when the examiner, in this case Mr Robertson, who from memory was the senior Maths lecturer at Jordanhill, comes out and watches you teach to see if you can 'do it properly.'

Well, I had filled in all the pre-crit paperwork and emphasised to the examiner that the real class teacher had said there was utterly no chance of this class staying remotely quiet and getting on with the work.

Or so I thought.

Nowadays students get hit with all that excuse making deprivation and mental health bollocks that they have to adhere to and 'believe' in, in their pre-crit paperwork but ours was more informative and honest and it made a lot more sense.

It also allowed us to get our excuses in early.

So, the day of the crit came and Mr Robertson, the examiner came in to see me in action.

All set, good to go.

Books were issued, resources allocated, questions and queries answered and then literally, the kids all just got on with it.

And I did as we were supposed to do and trawled the class trying to help and advise, but I could easily have put my feet up and fallen asleep.

It was that easy. Everyone just got on with it.

The examiner looked over the notes I had given him about the 'problem class' etc. then looked over at me utterly coasting. He gave me the thumbs up, and everything was moving along absolutely fine.

That is, it was all going lovely and smoothly until one pupil said one little innocent thing. Something utterly innocuous along the lines of 'Can I borrow a rubber please?' or something.

There was no problem with that at all.

However, there was a right 'madam' in the class, who was the one with the biggest potential to kick off according to her teacher, and she was sitting right in front of him.

She turned round and in that kind of really loud shouty type of whisper which was emphasised by the extreme silence in the room, she made it crystal clear to him, 'Shhhhh. Can you no see Mr Bhattacharyya's having a crit. You not see that ya idiot? That old guy there's his tutor. He's got to like him. Jees, what are you like?'

Then she turned to the tutor and me, rolled her eyes, tutted several times and wagged her finger at the poor pupil behind her, then doing that two fingers at her own eyes, two fingers at him 'I'm watching you!!' type action.

'I'm on to you' she finished with, to the poor pupil.

I kind of wanted the ground to open up.

But the tutor was brilliant at the end of the lesson. I assured him that I hadn't bribed or threatened them to behave, which was the truth. He was absolutely fine about it. As far as he was concerned, if the pupils were so willing to help you out and to perform for you in front of him when it mattered then you had to be doing something right.

What a guy.

And he never mentioned pedagogies.

55 THE BATTLE OF CROSSLET ROAD

Dumbarton Academy sits on Crosslet Road.

The new school sits on the old site, but the main building is to the east end of the grounds unlike the old main building where my room was which sat at the very west end of the grounds, next to the tenements and reasonably close to the shops.

The staffroom we used was above the carpark and looked out onto Crosslet Road.

So, one lunchtime myself, Peter, Bob and Arthur were up in the staffroom. They were sitting at the small coffee table while I was standing warming myself on the old radiator under the window.

Suddenly there was some commotion outside on the street.

I looked round and there were about four 'worthies' shouting abuse at a group of pupils from our school.

These four who were approaching from the right (west) were pupils that I didn't recognise.

'Come here and see this,' I said to the room.

The guys came over and we all gathered round the window to see what was going on.

Arthur said, 'I don't recognise any of them either,' and the rest agreed. But just as we were about to do the right thing and sensibly ignore any interruptions to our lunch hour (which, come to think of it must have been in itself somewhat of a rarity in that we were not in the games hall playing football) there was another different assortment of yelling and abuse as about twenty of our own 'home grown worthies' suddenly appeared from behind the gym on the left and gave chase down the street after the original four.

'Bloody hell, we need to do something.' I said and there was semi frantic agreement this time from Arthur and Peter.

But not so from Bob. He remained perfectly still.
You see, apparently ex-mercenary soldiers have a sort of sixth sense, second site type ability.

'Just wait,' he said. 'Just hold on and watch. Hold and watch.'

And sure enough the four 'visitors' were indeed indicating that they were in no sort of danger whatsoever. They simply jogged backwards to the right, outnumbered as they were about 5 to 1.

'And hold it,' Bob stated slowly and firmly, but calmly.

And as our twenty got to within about ten yards of the four unknowns, ready for war, out came perhaps eighty or ninety reinforcements from what became apparent was the other school in Dumbarton. Our guys had been classically lured and ambushed.

'And there you have it,' Bob said.

It was hilarious.

Of course, Bob had spotted this ambush straight away. That man has many talents, you know.
When I think about how well the other guys did, I have to ask, was Bob secretly teaching the other side 'manoeuvres', or worse.

Is there **another** mercenary somewhere out there in Dumbarton?

56 TRAVELLING WITH A NAME LIKE MINE

I think that over the years I must have become known to many people due to working in the school. Well, that reason mainly, but what many people don't know is that I also spent four months working in the Roads department in the council buildings at Garshake Road beforehand.

My dad also worked in a different branch of the roads department so by the time I started working at the academy it was not uncommon for parents at parents' nights beginning the interaction with 'You're Davy Bhattacharyya's boy, aren't you?' Fortunately, he was well thought of so that set me off on a good footing.

But the combination of my unusual name and knowing a great number of pupils does sometimes rear itself in relatively unusual and sometimes, surreal situations.

It's very common to be out and about with my wife or mates and literally bump into people I know through having taught them.

It's quite hard to place them sometimes as surnames mean so little and so many have the same first names but after a bit of reminiscing about who, what, where, when etc I can usually place them and so far, so good, it's always been ok.

And fortunately, no one has decked me yet.

But the most unusual meeting took place not in Glasgow, not in the UK but was actually in New York. Ivana and I had gone out to the Parlour bar way up on a hundred and somethingth street. It looked really good, and we went in, and I went up to the bar with Ivana standing next to me. I bought the drinks and had just handed Ivana hers when the barmaid suddenly screamed 'Ivana, hiiiieeee. It's me.' I can't remember her name, but it turned out that 'Me' had been to university with my better half.
So, then Ivana said, 'This is Bappi,' etc then introduced me as her husband, and revealed she was now Bhattacharyya rather than Favaretto.
And then in the most surreal moment ever, the guy at the other end of the bar who was also serving drinks turned to me and shouts 'Hey Mr Bhattacharyya, you taught me at Dumbarton!!'

These two didn't really know each other but each knew one of us. It would be nice to think they got together one day. Good times.

But meeting pupils and ex-pupils out of school can have its uses too.

We had been out at the Bon accord at Charing Cross in Glasgow, on a staff night out and it was time for me to leave to get what was probably the last train home. I realised John Christie (remember, the famous techie teacher and Friday lunchtime drinking buddy of mine) was a little bit worse for wear (of course, it must have been due to something he ate!!) and I wasn't sure if he could get a later train to Dumbarton where he lives quite near to the school, so I sort of dragged him along to the station. Fortunately, I was relatively fine, but he was six sheets to the wind and was walking on autopilot.

Anyway, we managed to get to the station and carefully got down to the platform.

The train arrived and I was somehow able to get him onto the train.

But then he fell asleep.
Totally out cold, sound asleep.

Now my stop is about five or six stops before his so I had to make sure he would get off ok.

The train was quite busy, so I shouted down the carriage, 'Is anyone getting off at Dumbarton?'

'Awright Mr B how you doing?'

No idea who or how many but there were plenty who seemed to know me.

'Listen, I've got Mr Christie here, can someone get him off the train at Dumbarton Central?' I asked, forgetting for a moment which of the stations he used.

'Naw, it's Dumbarton East he gets off at. No worries, Sir, we get him home all the time,' he informed me and that was that. 'A bad curry again sir, I take it?'

'Yeah, something like that!!'

Anyway, John was safe in the hands of these ex-pupils of the Academy.

Sometimes it's not so useful to be recognised, however.

There was a perception that I drank a lot. To be honest I did drink but not much more, if at all than anyone else - OK?

But in the pupil's minds a thought begins and unless extinguished immediately starts to grow (fester is probably a better word) until it becomes a ridiculous belief upon which everything else is based.

One day which I think must have been the last day of term, I was sent down to the high street to buy mineral water as there must have been some end of term presentation on. I ran round to the high street as this must have been before Asda and Morrisons built their superstores up the road and in the process helped destroy the High Street.
I got to Haddow's, which for those younger readers was the booze shop at the time, a rival to Vikky wine. It was 10-45 and the shop was only just opening with the big metal shutters half down across the door and window.

But I was on a tight deadline, so I bent down and started banging on the door just under the metal shutter shouting for service which wasn't a legal problem as the shop was allowed to sell alcohol only after 11am but anything else was allowed beforehand. They just had little custom at this time.

But as I'm kneeling down on the ground, half covered by the metal shutter and trying to shout for service, around the corner came one of the pupils in my class.

With her mother.

'Morning Mr Bhattacharyya.' they both said.

And just walked on without further comment.

57 THE JOURNEY HERE

As I said at the beginning of this book, I have a reasonably unique career path which gives me a real insight into Dumbarton Academy. At time of writing, I am currently on my fourth period of working there so a little bit of background and explanation may help you understand why?

I was first placed there when I received a phone call on a Friday afternoon in August 1989 by Strathclyde Regional Council which is: -

    a. An entirely random event

    b. A very fortunate event

As you will hopefully remember, I started on 'maternity leave' for a retired man and my temporary contract got extended then was made permanent.

However, the first change occurred after a couple of years when I was made surplus by the arrival in our school of Jim Turkington as an assistant head teacher who sadly for me was also a maths teacher.

So that was me out, and I got sent to Kirkintilloch High School.

Kirkie High was ok. It was quite a nice school if truth be told, and most of the pupils were really quite pleasant and fairly decent.

I also worked there with two 'off the scale brilliant' maths teachers, namely, Jane Gordon who was the Principal Teacher and Anne Horrocks the Assistant Principal Teacher, (by the way, a position that should never have been removed from Maths and English departments and probably others as well).

Anne was without doubt, the best teacher of any subject that I have ever encountered.

She was quite simply utterly outstanding.

Everything she said just made perfect sense and every pupil passed any level she taught and remember back then it was genuine assessment not the cheating which passes nowadays for internal assessment.

She is the reason I am very reluctant to change any of my teaching methods and to be honest if any of my pupils from yesteryear somehow managed to see me teach nowadays it really wouldn't be that different to how they perhaps remember it themselves.

I am not claiming to be remotely as good as she was, but she taught me what to do, what works, and what doesn't work and to my absolute thrill, she actually said I was good at it. High praise indeed but in hindsight she was maybe just being kind.

Kirkintilloch was ok, but it wasn't that exciting. My mates were all back at Dumbarton so when Arthur phoned me in my second year there to ask if I wanted to come back, I jumped at the chance. The lady at the council was very kind and claimed to know me personally which was fortunate as she pulled some strings which meant the one-year automatic return limit was overlooked and I got my old position in Dumbarton Academy back.

It's probably the next few years where most of the wilder tales in this book come from, but anyway, I stayed a few years but then got a bit restless. I had friends who worked for Pharmaceutical companies, and I fancied a bit of that myself.

So, after a few interviews I ended up working for a terrific company called Merck Pharma.

Funnily enough one of the things that helped me most was that many of the senior customers i.e. Consultants and Prescribing Advisers really engaged with me, more so than many other younger reps and seemed impressed that I had already had a career in education. A fellow professional no less.
By the way, this is worth remembering when, as a profession ourselves, we sometimes feel unworthy compared to other jobs and careers. While there are those who go on about the holidays etc there are a lot of people out there who are very grateful for the work that teachers do.

Moving forward, things went well, and I got head-hunted to join an even better company called Aventis.
I was very fortunate yet again, in that my boss (the head-hunter), a guy called Roger Morrison, was simply the best boss you could imagine working for. He made us work as he called it, in the 'grey' areas of sales.
Not illegal by any means but gently pushing the boundaries of legality if you get my drift. (You can see why we got on so well!) Top bloke, I am very grateful to him.

He is from Northern Ireland, and I definitely want to record it in writing that the people from Northern Ireland are quite simply just better than the rest of us. Go and work for one of them, you'll understand.

But he moved on and I ended up working in a different team. It was fine but not as good, and in a period of personal disruption while I was trying to move to a medical devices company which is really quite difficult, I got to speaking with Arthur again and I sort of ended back at you know where, this time being my third occasion.

The last couple of changes were when our head teacher at the time, quite unnecessarily in my opinion decided to make a colleague of mine Dan surplus and it was red rag to a bull with me, so emphasising my commitment to always 'back my mates', I went instead.

To Clydebank high school.

It was a bit of a culture shock mainly because it is so big compared to Dumbarton.

I was warned about joining the maths department there, but as far as I'm concerned, they were all brilliant and very welcoming to me, as well as being a very hard-working bunch.

I really liked them and thought they were all terrific. I also ended up with one really brilliant class there too. I strongly suspect they would have fitted in well in 'old school' Dumbarton. I genuinely enjoyed working with that class.

But Clydebank is a little close to where I live, and a few pupils seemed to 'know' my son Sam so when an opportunity to go to Port Glasgow High School arrived, I took it.

And that probably wasn't the wisest thing I've ever done.

Most of the department were really decent, as were most of the pupils and it's a school that certainly punches way above its weight in terms of results, but I was screwed over big time when I first arrived in terms of the timetable and by getting dumped with loads of the really dodgy classes, one in particular which the current teacher, at the time, just couldn't wait to get rid of.

The first few months were living hell until Covid jumped in and sorted it all.

Thanks China!!

For the next two years apart from two or three really nasty shit-stirring staff (one depute, one pastoral care) who made up all sorts of spurious rubbish and tried to cause problems between me and my classes, who, on the whole I really liked and got on well with, and a couple of utterly vile pupils (not the ones I hate btw, these idiots don't even come close) all was fine and the new Principal teacher who took over, Ronnie is yet another I can file under Genuine Privilege to work for.

Great guy. What a shift that guy puts in.

The two main miscreants in that place are cleaners Eunice and Bridie.

They are utterly wasted as cleaners in my opinion. These two are mental.

Especially Bridie.

The pair of them should be on the stage or TV.

I made the mistake of jokingly telling Bridie the old story that if someone asks me what I do for a living I tell them I'm a paedophile (I'm not of course). It's just that I'm far too embarrassed to say I'm a teacher. So what did she do? In front of the whole school, she shouted across the canteen 'Hey Paedo!!!' at me.

She wasn't born with an off switch.

Still love her though. She's wonderful. She had Ronnie and I in stitches on a daily basis. And she swears like a trooper.

But then finally an opportunity arose to go back and work at Dumbarton and of course, I applied for it.

I still had to go through an interview which was my first meeting with the new Head teacher Alison, and I had to be interviewed by both her and the senior depute Graham Mackay as well as my good friend and current head of maths, Anne Pacher.

It was really difficult trying not to make eye contact with Anne during the interview with me bullshitting away and Anne asking 'sensible' questions, as if I had done, then no doubt, we would both have buckled and been rolling around on the floor in tears of laughter.

But anyway, for whatever kind reasons, Alison ignored all petitions and other sensible advice against employing me and so I'm back.
Session number 4, and that's you up to date.

Being back I must have hit some sweet spot in terms of ages of pupils and their parents. The first few weeks were a procession of pupils coming into my class with messages from their parents who I had taught. It certainly helps with behaviour, and it's been really fun being back 'home'.

There's a granny story in there too and I'll tell you that one in the next chapter.

Don't worry.

It's not as bad as you think!!

58 GRANNIED

Actually it so totally is!!

Well, this one definitely has a time stamp all over it. It's very recent and takes place in Session 4 of my time at Dumbarton. That's definitely true but it overlaps with Session 2 as you're about to find out.

Remember I said before, on my return to Dumbarton after coming 'home' from Port Glasgow, that I was inundated with greetings and messages from pupils telling me that their mums and dads, uncles, and aunts etc were asking for me?

Well, I stopped digging too much as it became apparent the conversation at home had gone something along these lines.

'How did you get on at school today?'
'Fine'
'Really? Don't go into too much detail there about it'. I'm paraphrasing of course, but some of the pupils are boys after all.
'It was ok. Got a new teacher. Old guy. Laughs at his own jokes. Funny name.'
'That sounds like an old maths teacher I used to have years ago, what was his name? Mr Bhattacharyya?'
'Yeah, that's him'.
'You serious? I can't believe he's still Teaching/Alive.'
Take your pick.

That's the way I was led to believe how most conversations went and in some ways it's nice to be able to contribute to the bonds of communication and social interaction between teenager and stressed parents. As a parent, I can relate to this.

But anyway, the follow up was always pretty positive and either they genuinely remembered me reasonably fondly or were from an earlier time when folk were generally just a little bit more polite perhaps!!

However, there was one particular conversation that had a bit of a twist to it. I'll definitely not name this pupil, but after being back for a couple of days, this really nice young girl who wasn't actually in my class came up to me in the corridor, told me who she was and asked me if I remembered her mother. I genuinely did remember her mother and I remembered her really well. In fact, I'm pretty sure that she was one of the class we inflicted Professor Bon Jovi on many years back.

'Brilliant, tell your mum I said Hi,' etc.

But then I remembered something.

'Hold on.' I said. 'How's your gran doing?'

'Whaaaaat?'

Right, so let me take you (the reader) back to session 2. To make this easier to follow we will call the three characters in this tale Pupil, Mum and Mum's mum. Get it?

Ok. Well back in session 2, I taught Mum maths and Peter taught Mum English. There had been a parents' evening back then which, as ever, ran well into the evening and despite this, Mum's mum had not attended to talk about Mum. You still with me?

So, Peter and I got informed that we had to wait behind after school to see this, in our totally unjust opinion, what we considered to be, lazy, opportunistic 'charlatan' who was happy to use up 'our' time instead of her own. Really professional of us both. I think what really annoyed us was that it was only the two of us who had to wait behind at the end of the day. No other teachers.

Incandescent with completely unmerited rage we swore that Peter would 'only' see her 3-30 to 3.36 then bring her to my room and I would 'only' see her for the next six minutes. Peter and I travelled in to work together so we were both doubly inconvenienced.

So, I waited in my room.

3-36 came and went.

3-46 did the same.

3-56 hurtled by too.

In fact, it was sometime after 4-00 that Peter came down to my room with Mum's mum and the reason for the tardiness suddenly became more than apparent.
It was absolutely crystal clear.

You see Mum's mum would easily have given any super model a run for their money. She was stunning. She was also wearing some kind of tight gym gear too, which was possibly down to the fact that she was also a dance teacher. To cap it all, she even owned her own pub. It was no wonder she had spent so long with Peter. He couldn't believe his luck and without the slightest doubt had been flirting and trying it on mercilessly with her.

And I don't blame him.

I did exactly the same. She was absolutely wonderful, and she was a great laugh too. Peter and I are of course a couple of the biggest hypocrites you will ever meet. Guilty as charged.
Lines like 'Pop in any time, any help you need etc.'

We were utterly shameless.

So back to the present and I related a version of this story to pupil (granddaughter) who straightaway went home and told her mum and phoned her gran i.e. Mum's mum to let her know too.

Apparently, she expressed a degree of incredulity that I was:

A- Still Teaching
B- Still Alive.

I love that tale because it links two or rather in this case three generations of Dumbarton people and each one of them is someone it has also been a privilege to know and / or work with.

One last thing about 'Grannies.'

I believe it is very common for students at universities who have not been able to meet a deadline for an essay to claim the sudden demise of a grandparent and thus gain an extension.

I have it on *outstandingly* good authority that a really difficult essay can somehow cause Armageddon in the geriatric world.

You have to ask why the essays are so dangerous for old folks.

And why this happens SO often to trainee TEACHERS.

59 BELT UP

When people of a certain generation think of schools and their own school days, school discipline probably sits close to the forefront of their minds. Let me just put it out there that schools are nothing like what they were in the times before this book but even over the relatively short timescale described in these chapters it has changed and adapted enormously. It would be quite contentious for me to put my opinions about what I think of the way things have headed recently in terms of discipline, but you will probably get a better idea of my thoughts about it generally with a few stories and anecdotes relating to it.

Well firstly when I started teaching, 'the belt' had been pretty much banned and that alone causes a great deal of debate in itself.
I have always had quite good discipline in my classes, and I think that's mainly to do with a combination of humour and showing respect to pupils and by that, I mean genuine respect. Sadly, there are an awful lot of teachers who are quick to promote Respect and Values etc but when you dig a little bit deeper, they are all talk.

How do I know this?
Literally the evidence of hundreds of pupils over the years.

As I said, and the tales seem to back this up, I do like humour and banter in a class. Nowadays, humour is something that officialdom almost frowns upon in case it causes offence.

Of course, it causes offence, that's the point. Does it cause or encourage nastiness? No, of course not. That's the difference. Also, humour and banter work both ways. Simple rule I have is that if I can say X to a pupil, they can say X back to me i.e. it is mutual and works both ways. It certainly works well in Dumbarton, perhaps less so elsewhere.

Like every teacher on Earth, mine goes wrong sometimes. Here's a few situations which prove the point.

John (Marti Pellow from the Bon Jovi tale) was a student teacher who was in our department way back in early nineteen ninety something. He was working with me in my class and was taking a pretty decent class I had, S1/S2 from memory. This class were all pretty good but there was one pupil you could file under 'bat-shit crazy.' What is noticeable is that at that time he stood out. I'm not sure if he would remotely stand out now.
Anyway, John was having a real problem with him, getting him to settle etc and so I said to John to watch and see how I dealt with him.

It was Friday, last period of the day.
The conversation went something along these lines after the pupil as per usual had done something annoying or just daft.
'You, out now!' I bellowed. Now, I don't tend to shout or raise my voice very much, so when I do it is particularly noticeable.
The urchin came out with an apologetic and sheepish look.
I positioned him at the open door just inside the corridor mainly for John's benefit.
And then I went through him. I went into real hairdryer territory.

It ended up with..."It's Friday, it's last period. Do you think I want to be stuck in here with you? Do you? No, I want to get out of here, I want to get to the football, I want to get to the pub and see my mates. Do you think I want to spend time dealing with you?'

And with that, and dealing with what must have been in his mind, the most relative aspect of my diatribe and key element of my argument, the urchin looked up (angelically) and said, 'Are you a good footballer Sir?'

Just like that he had totally destroyed my rant. I hadn't actually been annoyed at the start but was ready to kill him when I got into full flow. I just stood there gawping as he then smiled, and actually thanked me, before he went back into the room and casually returned to his seat.

And John winked and said, 'Ah right. So that's how you deal with him.'

Sometimes, however, humour develops of its own accord, and you are powerless to deal with it. Just embrace it is my advice to any potential new teacher.

There was one pupil who kicked off about something in the old school, I cannot remember what, but it ended up with him storming out of the class (remember this was back when that sort of thing was discouraged, now it's almost a suggestion to prevent 'mental illnesses for many kids from the idiot squad that exist, somewhere in the nether world of education nowadays.)

Anyway, this kid got up and stormed out, being really abusive to me as he went, and on his way out, he attempted to slam the door but what he didn't realise was the door opened both in the way *and* out the way, so it just gently oscillated around the middle a couple of times.

I chased him to the door as by now I was quite annoyed, so as he reached the fire doors, just up the corridor, I insulted him with something along the lines of 'You can't even slam the door properly.'

So, with a face full of raging fury he tried to slam the fire doors.

Which   closed   really   really   really   slowly!
He ended up trying to push them closed with his shoulder which was obviously quite hysterical as it didn't work either and so we had a moment where he just looked at me in utter despair. To be honest he looked about ready to cry.

I looked back at him and then it happened. The two of us just bent double and started roaring with laughter. I think it ended up a great solution. He came back in and was the perfect child after that, but he did take serious dog's abuse about not being able to slam a door.

And the other main tale about picking your battles involves one of my very favourite pupils of all time. I'm not going to name him as he is sadly not around any more to offer his permission for this.

But anyway, what you have to know is that although he was a great pupil, he wasn't the most academic, but he was not as bad as his voice (low, deep, slow drawl kind of thing) implied.

Well, let's just say that he had a tendency to swear.

Not in that idiotic pretend Tourettes sort of way, but just as a way of likening unto a comma, separating every other two or three words in any sentence.

No malice intended at all.

Or no 'Fu****g malice intended at all,' as he would probably have put it better himself.

He obviously had the hots for one of the girls in the class, but she and her friend were acting up in that grey area that lies somewhere between being really not interested in his potential advances, and totally leading him on.
I felt quite sorry for him.

But the problem was, he just wouldn't stop swearing. It was relentless.
So eventually I threatened to put him out of the class.
Which worked for about 45 seconds or so.

Then I **had** to put him out of the class.

But he kept opening the door and begging to get let back in. He complained he had been out there 'for ages.'
In truth, he had only been out of the room about a minute and a half.

So eventually I relented, went out and tried to reason with him.
'Please Mr B, please let me back in.'
'I can't until you stop swearing.'
'Ah promise ah'll no swear, honest tae ****'
'What?'
'Naw please man, she's talking aboot me in there.'

'I can't let you til you stop swearing.'
'She's fryin' ma nut Mr B.'
'Ok so promise you'll not swear again if I let you back in.'
'No man Ah pure promise man.'
'Ok. in you go.'
I opened the door and let him back in.
'Haw (name of girl) get out ma f*****g seat.'
'Aw f**k' sorry sir'
'Oh s**t' didn't mean tae f*****g swear, ya ba****d.'

Well, what can you say?

In my case, very little as I was on my knees on the floor buckled with laughter (again) watching this battle going on between his brain and his vocal chords.

To be honest, there is a lesson in there somewhere but I'm not sure I'm clever enough to know what it is, and so my advice to any new teacher would be to learn to pick your battles.

Don't back yourself into a corner and remember the behaviour is not usually directed at you. Be flexible.

He was a fantastic pupil. A genuine good guy.

As a sort of footnote to his tale, a few years back some kids came in after lunch and said that a guy sitting on the wall outside the Meadow Centre (Sports centre) had been asking for me.

I asked who it was and none of them knew.

Then one of them did the perfect impression. 'He just said "Haaawww gonae tell Mister B he's a f*****g great c**t.'

I've no *proof* it was him of course but the colourful linguistics make me suspect that it almost certainly was.

I started this section talking about the belt. Let me just add one last thing to that.

For years Peter had a belt (or was it two?) hanging up in his hall. You will have to ask him yourself if you want to know why but most people are happy to explain it away with the line. 'Well, you know, that's just big Peter for you.'

But anyway, why am I telling you this? Well one night at a party up at his flat we had all had a few and I got around to taking one of the belts off the wall and saying to Bob really smugly, 'C'mon Bob, let's see how good you were.'

Again, it's really not one of the most sensible choices I've ever made, and, in his defence, Bob did offer me several 'outs' before I stuck my hands out in front of him.

Well Bob did that shuffle/twitch type thing he does, looked me in the eye, apologised with his eyebrows raised, then brought all Hell down on my right hand. Bloody hell, it was like his own version of the Enola Gay's infamous cargo landing on my hand. I swear my extended relatives on the sub-continent must have looked at each other saying 'What the f**k was that?'

But then he did Peter so that made it all worthwhile.

Bob Johnston armed with a belt does explain a thing or two, doesn't it?

Footnote: When Bob retired, he gave me his belt, he left it in the drawer for me with the message To Bappi, best wishes, Bob.

I gave it to my mate Tom.

You see, Tom collects weapons.

60 POGWATCH

In recent years there has been a tendency for new temporary promoted positions to be created in schools. These are given titles like 'Teacher for Raising Attainment, Teacher for Diversification, Teacher for Liaison with whatever.'

They do however get referred to in staff rooms and bases as for example 'The Minister for Paper Clips' and the like.

No one really knows what most of these positions are all about including often the very people doing the actual jobs but as there are few promoted positions available especially if you are in a bigger department, I can see why people go for these jobs. And good luck to them.

But invariably it's my female colleagues who go for and get the vast majority of these positions, and quite often, it's the very new teachers. They are often not yet at the top of the regular pay scale even though there are only about five bands, so they pretty much go straight onto Point One of the Promoted pay scale.

Selfishly I used to put the two facts together and the term Point One Girl was formed, or POG for short. People started talking about POG jobs as well.

But in one of the other schools, I worked in, I was in the staff room one day when one of the teachers who was high up in one of the unions came in knotting himself.

It turns out at the National Union conference or whatever similar event it was, someone from far far away had used the actual expression POG job and when his colleagues had questioned what it meant our guy was fortunately in a position to explain this new term to them.

I like to think that is my main contribution to the world of teacher discussion, but perhaps there is a like-minded person somewhere out there and they also came up with the very same expression.

And, you never know, maybe they've written a book too!

61 BEST ANSWER EVER

You encounter some real characters amongst the pupils. It's strange as sometimes the various eccentricities are hilarious and endured or welcomed by everyone whilst others get filed under the term 'weirdo.'

Nowadays there is an obvious one which is very topical across whole sections of society, but I won't be tilting at that particular windmill in case of accusations of hate crime. The King most certainly is in the Altogether. That's all I'll say about that issue.

But two particularly unusual ones come to mind. At Dumbarton I had a pupil who was a really nice kid, but he obviously had his own issues. He was very focussed and fixed on what he did in class and remember, apparently sometimes that's considered a bad thing. I liked him, however.

He had the really strange trait that every so often he would talk in a particular accent, French, German etc but best of all when he hit Italian and nota justa regular Italian, I mean full on Super Mario levels of the language of love.
Professional as always, I used to joke with him about it and if we hadn't heard from 'The Italian' in a while I would always ask for him and try to find out when he was coming back to see us again. In other words, I ripped it right out of him.

But then he really started to shy away any time I mentioned it and we went months without this character being around.

Until that is, the day he almost burst into the classroom.
'Heyyyyy, Guessa who's backa?' he bellowed.

'The Italian!!! Howa you doing my man? Howa the devil are you and a wherea you been?' I replied in my best impression of my late Father-in-law.

All was good. Really good. Until I checked my emails later, after the lesson. I don't know if the timing was relevant or not, but the poor kid had been diagnosed as having some kind of multiple personality disorder.
At this point I really panicked. 'Don't draw attention,' was the basis of the instruction and yet I had literally been serenading him in the class.

Worriedly, I went to see his guidance teacher, Carol, who was a friend and someone I could trust, looking at whether I should phone his mum and apologise etc before there was a complaint in against me (which would have been well deserved in this case). Carol, being Carol just looked at me then immediately burst out laughing.

'Oh yes.' she says sarcastically, 'You, of all people are going to get a complaint. Yeah, right! Yours is the ONLY bloody class I can get him to go to and then get him to STAY in. He absolutely loves going to Maths.'

So, there you have it. The unconventional approach is sometimes the best.

But there was another pupil at another school I taught who although terrific was in many ways uniquely strange. He used to wear a deerstalker hat around the school but that only tells part of the story. I ended up getting his class (which I liked) allegedly since no one else in the department could put up with him. (Not true by the way.) I consider that a win.

But his outstanding reply to me was when I had the temerity to ask him why he wore this unconventional headwear to school.

'Well Sir.' He talked quite puckerfully, 'It's just that I thought that the top hat with the purple feather would look rather silly, don't you think, what?'

Although he was a 'real character' he also got a bit nervous so before one of his exams I did try to motivate him to help and reassure him.
I said to him. 'Listen.'

'You're stronger than you seem.'
'You're braver than you believe.'

Then I added.

'And you're smarter than you look.'

'Oh, I say, that's very kind of you Sir.'

Totally nuts he was. But an absolutely top bloke at the same time.

62 SPIRITING UP THEIR INTEREST

Well, I hope by now you not only have enjoyed the tales of merriment and nonsense, all true I feel obliged to remind you, but on the off chance that any teachers or potential teachers take a butcher's at this nonsense then hopefully there are a few tips to be gotten along the way.

This one deals with getting pupil's interest.

The lesson was on something about circles. Yes, bloody circles. Possibly the most boring part of the maths curriculum and sure enough the class were overwhelmed with boredom and intransigence at the thought.

So, I drew a circle on the board. The class showed the requisite amount of disinterest to this.

Then I made a circle on the empty front desk, out of whatever was to hand at the time.

'Hey, guys, does this not look like we're setting up for a Ouija board?' I said.

'Someone might need to keep an edgy.' (a lookout)

And it got me the desired response.

'Sir, have you ever done a Ouija board?'

Dramatic pause.

'I don't want to talk about it.'

And with that I had their undivided attention. No doubt, a real professional would have used the silence to negotiate for the story to be related *after* the lesson, but an idiot like me doesn't think like that. I have priorities. It was all brewing nicely in my mind.

'Go on, what happened?'

'Can't talk about it.' Hands at this point raised, palms facing the class, trying to be seen to not breathe normally.
'Pleeeeeease.'

More dramatic pause.

'Ok then.'

'Well, you know how I was trying to sell my flat?'

All kids start nodding slowly in agreement at this apparently commonly known piece of information. I have no idea why that was the case as firstly I had never mentioned any housing transactions to them ever, and secondly, I wasn't planning on selling my flat, but remember nodding and pedantic detail etc. Go for it and they lap it right up.

'Well remember I told you that I'm selling my flat and I'm trying to move to a bigger one (Of course I hadn't, and I wasn't but, as we've discussed many times now, it's the pedantic detail that sells it).

Much nodding.

'Well, just the other night me and my mates had been doing a Ouija board, for a laugh like. Anyway, we had all the letters out and we put off the lights and stuff. And of course, we all started to do swear words and stuff.'

More pause for effect. Eyes closed for several seconds.

'No, I can't go on, let's get back to circles. What's a diameter?'

No way was this even remotely going to take place. They were all on the spiky barbed bit end of the line and they were tonight's protein supplement to the chips.

'Noooo, tell us what happened.'
'Phew, ok. Well then, suddenly there was a breeze, but all the windows and doors were shut, and then we all heard a sort of moaning sound. It's hard to describe but we all heard it.'

'Then the glass started moving around the letters itself with our fingers still on it, but no one was pushing, and then it started to spell out a word.

'What did it say?'

T.   T.   Roberts.' For maximum suspense I said this really, really, slowly.

Even more pause for more effect

'Well remember I said I wanted to move to Dennistoun? Cause it's cheaper to get a two-bedroom flat there?' (Again, never said a thing about this at all to them)

Nodding much slower now. They were all hardly breathing. I suspect that a good surgeon could have removed their spleens without any of them noticing, they were all that caught up in the story.

'Well, I saw a flat in the paper that was for sale in Dennistoun, and I went round to buy it,' (yeah, cause that's how it's done of course) but when I got to the close, I looked at the names and one of them said...'

And at this stage every single one silently mouthed 'T. T. Roberts'.

'Yeah,' I whispered, 'That's exactly what it said, T. T. Roberts.'
'So, what did you do?'
'I ran. In fact, I ran like the wind. I'd have given Jesse Owens a run for his money, I ran that fast.'

'So, what happened?'

'Well later on, about half an hour after I ran away, there was a big gas explosion. The flat blew up. If I'd been in there paying for the house, you guys would have a different maths teacher now.'

There was a collective 'Awwwwwwwww.' Pause.

In a virtual whisper. 'Now let's look at circles'.
And with that we began to discuss diameters and radii and for whatever reason, that day they paid unusually high levels of attention.

By the way, I have no idea who T T Roberts is or may be, but remember Tom, my mate from earlier, well it just so happens his surname is Roberts.

63 THE BOB JOHNSTON SCALE OF LEARNING

Here's another tip:-

Since we are now looking at aspects of teaching where a new teacher may perhaps learn something themselves let's look at what we call the Johnston Scale of Learning.

If you are asked 'How many times on average do you need to tell a pupil something before they remember it?' you will no doubt get a multitude of responses.

The universities say it must be less than three as doing more than three of the same type of example breaches pupils' human rights, or something just as daft. But, as I've grown to realise, the people who come up with this garbage are idiots.

And as we know:-

Universities contain many idiots.

Universities contain many idiots.

Universities contain many idiots.

See, they won't remember it so I'm fine and it kind of proves my point.

No, according to the great creator of the Johnston Scale of Learning himself the answer is actually 500.

The scale itself looks something like this.

1-5 times.
Not worth mentioning.

6-20 times.
Remember you being in the room but unfortunately pupils can't actually remember anything you said.

21-100 times.
Vague recollection of topic.

101 - 300 times.
Starting to trigger something. Not sure what though.

300-400 times.
Remind me again, maybe just one more time.

400-499 times.
It's on the tip of my tongue.

500
Total recall. Get in there!

Sadly however, there exists a 501+ times entry.

Damn, forgotten it.

The Johnston Scale of Learning should be one of the first items any trainee teacher learns before entering a classroom.

64 OUT OF THIS BLACK AND WHITE WORLD

Two stories here.

First one.
It must have come up in conversation with a class about some old black and white picture.
So, the girl at the front says, 'How come it's in black and white?'

Ok that's fine. But she follows it up with, 'See back years ago, was the world just black and white?'

I kid you not. That is exactly what she asked me.
It's not as daft as the question in the next story but stick with this just now.
This was too good an opportunity to miss.

'Sure, it was,' I said. 'Everything in the whole world used to be just black and white.'
The class are all rolling their eyes but as she sat at the front of the class, she didn't see them, and she seemed to be buying it.
'Yeah, I remember the night they told us the world would be in colour the next day. It was dead exciting. You could hardly sleep.

And then in the morning it was brilliant, you just went out and the sky was blue, and the grass was green. Even though we didn't know what these words meant it was brilliant.'

On a roll now, I continued.

'You know what the only problem was? It was what we were all wearing. You suddenly found out that clothes that had been just light grey or dark grey were all sorts of different colours. I was wearing pink jeans and yellow top.'
'Actual?'
'Yes. Have any of you heard of a program called swap shop?'
Surprisingly some of them had.
'Well, that got set up so we could swap our lime green shoes with our bright red shirts and things.'
As I said, she seemed quite happy with this explanation.

The other genius in question (different class, different time) started off her question 'Is Africa…'

Now that's fine if it's followed up with the words 'far away' or 'somewhere you have been to', or even at a push, 'a country,' but no, this space cadet finished with the words 'on this planet?'

Seriously. She wanted to know if Africa was on the same planet as the one, she lived on.

I didn't have an answer for that.

In hindsight I wish I had asked her where she thought her previous teacher, Dr Mekwi (that we talked about earlier) was from. He was from Cameroon.

Now this girl left school and went to university, probably studying something useful like Tasmanian Basket Weaving or Venezuelan Toe Art.

So there exists the possibility of a conversation something along these lines.

'Did you see that (e.g. Star trek) last night on TV?'

'Oh, I did'
'These extra-terrestrials were mental, weren't they?'
'Do you know that I got taught by an extra-terrestrial.'

As I say. Universities contain many idiots.

65 SNOW FUN BEING A PROFESSIONAL

The weather can make some difference to the education of pupils. As we have discussed earlier, the temperature can often vary between Tropical and Baltic and that can be in classrooms that are right next to each other.
Rain, Wind and even Sun can all affect how pupils perform in your class and a special mention must be awarded to whatever causes the effect that a full moon has on them.
However, without a shadow of a doubt the weather system that causes the most disruption to pupils is of course, Snow.

Snow is terrific. Don't get me wrong, I hate the bloody stuff. Thank goodness there is so much less (or is it more? – Sorry, I forget which is their CURRENT lie) of the stuff according to that Swedish non-attender Greetin' Greta.

By the way, I always feel that idiot could have done with staying on at school – well, at least until the afternoon!!!

But anyway, snow affects pupils the most.

Why?

Well, in perhaps not the way you think.

It's because, though we are all consummate professionals, at the first drop of the white stuff, we all claim danger to life and limb and roll back under our duvet.

Please note, I mean at our individual homes, under our own duvets. I read this back just there and it sounds as if all the staff live together in one big house and sleep in one big bed then roll over under one massive quilt. Bloody hell, perish that thought.

Nowadays since the advent of Microsoft Teams and Google Classroom there's a rather quaint game, we are compelled to play on these occasions in which we as staff have to put together work for all classes with videos and information to help with the multitude of questions which we also arrange for all the classes.

Why do I call it a quaint game?

Well, that's because parents have the right which they often use to complain if material is not available / suitable / clear / plentiful etc.

Whereas the pupils just ignore it.

It's like when a guidance teacher is forced to come and ask you for work for Mungo Johnny as he is off school with syphilis or something. You run about daft collecting work which gets sent home but it never actually 'quite' gets started.

You could literally put anything up online.
It won't get done.

But on snow days, staff like to pretend in various online group chats (WhatsApp etc) that we are all ready to brave the elements Captain Scott style and make our way to our grand seats of learning. Cause we don't want 'our' pupils to miss out.

Well, that is if management are on that particular chat group. If they aren't then there seems to be a highly suspicious amount of praying hands and snowflake emojis etc. Just saying.

And quite right too. It's brilliant getting that extra day off. Like people in real jobs do!!

But sometimes you have to wait hours as the snow falls and starts to build up if you are unlucky enough to actually be in the school when the snow starts falling. This is to allow the health and safety people at the council (working from home no doubt) to make sure the roads are sufficiently treacherous before allowing you to leave early.

The worst time was when it took me nearly three hours to get home, a journey which usually takes about thirty minutes. At one point my car went into a beautiful spin and pirouetted a full 360 degrees, it must have looked tremendous, but it scared the shit out of me although perhaps that maybe had more to do with the double decker bus a few yards behind and by this time, hurtling towards me.

But it wasn't always like this. Not at Dumbarton anyway.

At one point we had a part time submarine commander who was the head teacher, yet another really good boss. He used to close the school at what felt like the merest hint of a minor frost.

In particular, there was one day when three snowflakes must have hit the ground in close proximity and so with 'Safety First' in mind, Dumbarton Academy was closed for the rest of the day. That was it, 9-45am, go home.

And, not needing to be asked a second time, we sort of scarpered out of the premises. Before we left, we all got a reminder that it was your professional duty and Strathclyde Regional Council official policy to go forth and find the closest 'open' educational establishment nearest to your house and to then work there for the day.

Yeah, that'll be 'Shining Bright'. Balls to that, we headed straight to (as you've probably guessed) Jinty's.

It was brilliant, we were passing all sorts of primary kids with snow over the tops of their wellies, and we were actually heading to the pub. You see, as I've told you over and over, we were professional through and through.

On this particular day there were four of us. Bob, Peter, myself and one other. I will not name him as it is unfair but I'm going to call him Scrooge. I think he may have been on supply. You see, he was literally as tight as a duck's arse, the kind of guy who could peel an orange in his pocket all the while wearing a boxing glove. Whenever we went to the pub he would 'hold the door,' or 'head to the toilet,' anything other than buy a round.

So, this day we had it all sorted.

I would get the door. It was 11.05 by the way.
Peter would go to the toilet.
Bob would need to go out and get cash.

This arrangement was cunningly and strategically thought out to force Mr Scrooge to be first up to the bar.
And to our extreme surprise, it actually worked.

Well, it seemed to work until the bugger produced, believe it or not, a hundred-pound note!! I think that was the first time I had ever seen one. And of course, at five past eleven in the morning what bar can give change for that?

I strongly suspect that he kept it for emergency situations like that one.

66 CHANGE – FOR BETTER OR FOR WORSE

When I started writing this gibberish, what seems like ages ago, it was mainly just for a bit of a laugh. It also allowed me to repeatedly use the nauseating phrase, 'I address this issue in my book,' endlessly to my colleagues so please let me first apologise for all that.

However, writing it has been strangely therapeutic and has brought back a ton of good memories. Now that it has been turned into a 'book' that people can actually buy, I have given some thought as to what to do on the off chance that any money is made.

I don't want it.

I've had too much fun doing this.
So, on the off chance someone buys it, all profits will go to three charities, *The Smile Train* as hopefully this book makes **you** smile, *Vision Aid* (come on, cataracts stopping kids see, that's outrageous in this day and age) and finally, the *Donkey Sanctury* as it's heartbreaking seeing images of these or indeed any animal suffering.

You could say the Success Criteria for this opus therefore are:-

-One kid who can smile
-One kid who can see
-One donkey living it up with a great big bag of carrots

The early indication of sales numbers do suggest we can raise enough money for a bag of carrots!

OK, way back, what seems ages ago, the title of Chapter 3 was The Times they are a Changin'.

So, as my career starts to wind down, as my working life races towards its own chequered flag, as the sun sets on my educational horizon and eventually I run out of these stupid cliches, I can no doubt look forward to the great and the good looking for a suitable field to put me out to pasture in, running wild and free, no doubt, with my good friends Bob, Arthur, Peter, and the eternally youthful John Christie, who (by the way, it is finally safe to reveal was even a teacher at my own school when I was a pupil. Sorry John!!)

Hey, just realised, I might even get to catch up with that Donkey too!!

But I'd finally like to end the book with a look at some changes over the years, the good and the bad.

Well let's start with this one.

Me.

To be honest I don't think I have changed too much. That's maybe to do with the fact that *'Age is compulsory whereas Maturity is entirely optional'.*

Oh, sure. I look much older and decrepit than I did when I started out, but to be honest, I have tried to stay completely true to my values. I still treat everybody with respect, all pupils, all teachers, all staff and all parents. If you don't, you're just a dick.

I still believe that bigots are an embarrassment, bullies should be shot and there's a special place in Hell for people who are cruel to animals.

My favourite film of all time is still Blazing Saddles, I still remain eternally optimistic that Brighton and Hove Albion will, one day, finally win something. In the 'who is the best Star Trek/ Star Wars,' argument, all I can say is Live Long and Prosper, and of course AC/DC still sound as fresh and brilliant as ever.

I also still have many of the notes and lessons from years ago but as with most things in the class in terms of lessons, it's all in my head.

I believe I still laugh at all of my own jokes as well, so I do mightily apologise for that too.

On second thoughts, no I don't. I love my own bad jokes. They're a keeper. They're staying.

And talking of 'thoughts', if this ever gets made into a film, as the credits are scrolling up slowly at the end, I want the third song on the Fun Boy Three album of the same name as the background music.

(Look it up on Spotify – you'll understand!!!)

Also, fundamental decency of Dumbarton the town is still the same, even though it's not immune to the ills of society which we seemed to have been able to avoid for so many years but are now increasingly plagued with. The vast majority of people (indeed as they are everywhere) are really decent, good sorts. I still have what I call the Wallet analogy.

What that means is that if I lost my wallet (again) more than 99% of pupils would return it intact.
Sadly, to be honest it's probably not as high as 99% nowadays but certainly 90 plus.

Our school is generally considered very positive by the likes of most students and probationers and another thing worth mentioning that I have always been really impressed with (especially in recent years, last decade or so) is that we recognise Holocaust Memorial day. We don't have any particular Jewish connection but it's great that our school recognises this important day and sadly, especially at this time of writing. Well done to whoever is all over that one.

My department are different of course to when I started out, but they are all great people and to be honest, put me to shame on a regular basis. It would be an interesting experiment to see what would happen if we swapped over a few between the ages. Who would like it? Who would hate it?

Dan Keany would have loved it back then. I'm convinced he was cloned in my first session (possibly by the Chemistry and Biology departments) and was just released back into modern society a few years back. Kind of like the Terminator in reverse.

Anyone who manages to sneak off to Liverpool on a Wednesday to go to a football match and gets past all the senior managers who each think he's working somewhere else in the building at the time is a borderline genius.

That and the fact that like me, he regularly used pupils' nicknames and mercilessly ripped it out of them for bad makeup or indeed virtually anything the daft kids ever said or did etc; it's excellent stuff.

We could tell we were quite like-minded in our approaches to education and that it would be 'nuts' to think we weren't going to get along splendidly, after our first conversation on his first day in the school!!

It's sad in a way that education can't hold on to the likes of Dan, not just cause he's my mate, but he's an outstanding teacher – well, not sad for Dan himself.

He's gone out rocking into the big world of Accountancy and he's already making big noises there.

I don't think Bob would like it as much now as he did back then.

Some of the things which have changed over the years have nearly destroyed education. The curriculum which is meant to offer more 'freedom' is so restrictive it's scary. The so called CfE capacities including the hilariously (en)titled 'Responsible Citizens' are all the very opposite of what they claim them to be for.

It feels Orwellian at times.
(Better buy this in paperback before it's cancelled.)

I feel my own subject, Maths, is in its death throes in this country. People can't do it, so they gradually run it down, ruin it, and one day, they'll remove it.

Exams are rare and farcical now despite the efforts of my hard-working colleagues. Why? Because the powers in Edinburgh can't do them, so discredit them, and will no doubt, finally, I fear, abolish them.

Pointless projects here we (you) come!

By the way, according to my mate who works in a university and is probably the most intelligent person I have ever met (not like the 'don't say it three times' brigade) the four capacities are all made up apparently by the bloke who got the contract to make the Scottish parliament mace.

Check it out, it's well hidden but it's true.

More recently, mobile phones have entered the discussion. Of course, they are a great thing but the addiction to them that pupils have is in my opinion really dangerous. I think it exacerbates all minor ailments and issues and ends up with a ridiculous number of pupils getting some sort of label etc. That nonsense is a growth industry in itself. Again, perhaps not accidentally.

Gentle suggestion for '*some*' parents; before you try to get your kid a mental health diagnosis, why don't you try taking their phone off them for a while and maybe booting them outside to get some fresh air. Perhaps even indulge in a little two-way conversation with them!! See what *might* happen if you try that first.

Also, another thing we are sadly in danger of losing, is camaraderie among staff.

Sure, back in the day, we all had a moan about certain departments e.g. no one wanted a class after they had been at French.

No criticism of that department, as to be honest they were probably one of, if not the best department in the school but the pupils were so enthused and engaged in those classes, they were almost wired by the time they came to your own class.

Getting them down from the ceiling (or MacUndoing them) was an art form of sorts.

Nowadays I feel there is a bit too much friction between departments, and I can't for the life of me understand teachers who can walk past each other in a corridor without saying 'Hello'. And unbelievably, we still have *some* teachers who think that they are somehow 'better' than the cleaners, janitors etc.

Really? Can we not just all respect everyone?

We have always been fairly lucky, in my opinion, at Dumbarton as well, in that the overwhelming majority of Head Teachers in the school have been really friendly and approachable. From speaking to other teachers in other schools, that is certainly not the case everywhere. There's one of course who wasn't but he's been away for a long time and he's not worth thinking about.

And of course, maths is still maths. Pythagoras' theorem is still the same, something to do with triangles, I think; Circles are still round, and I eventually found out why we use radians instead of degrees and what the other silly G setting means on a scientific calculator.

But generally, it's a pretty good job. It's not as easy as some members of the public make it out to be, but to be honest, it's also not nearly as bad as some of us profess it to be.
Most of the pupils are still reasonably willing to sit while we prattle on and certainly in Dumbarton they are usually up for a laugh.

I think Dumbarton is a great place and Dumbarton Academy is a superb place to earn your crust in. Even WDC are worth a shout out, they are all really easy to deal with and have been great to me. The fact that this is my fourth time working in the Academy would seem to confirm that I do quite like it there.

Well of course I do. I get to hang out with some of my friends every day and I have done for years and years.
I'm not going to sit and name them all, there are far too many.

One colleague I will mention is an old pupil of mine (who according to her mum hated me.
I don't blame her.
She assures me though; it was just the maths. OK, I'll believe you!) Anyway, we have put it behind us and now, Emma is yet another of my outstanding colleagues who somewhat brilliantly has created 'Cake Day.' It's such a simple, yet valuable and enjoyable experience (Basically it's getting about 8 billion mainly home-baked calories split between sixty or so staff - what's Not to like!!!) and it definitely makes Emma what I'd call, 'Old School.'

Take that as the ultimate compliment Emma.

I have always appreciated the help and support of the senior managers from day one, right up to the present, and I still feel that they always have your back. That is certainly not a given in all schools by the way.

They definitely, for whatever ridiculously kind reasons, have always had mine. Our current bunch are superb.

The pressure the likes of themselves, the excellent Guidance department and Support for Learning, Pupil and Family Support, my fellow departments, office colleagues, janitors and cleaners and my own outstanding maths colleagues (Anne, Brian, Shona, Donna, Joanne, Claire, Gill (ex-Techy, now Art, honorary Maths, really talented), Carol and Emma) are sometimes under, is ridiculous and I feel that it would break many lesser individuals.

By the way, I know at least Donna will laugh at this book.
That's because Donna laughs at anything! Anything at all.

Funnily enough, as I was driving in to work today, I remembered that I wanted to say that here. But then I remembered I had to add a bit to the AC/DC chapter.

So to help me remember as I was driving, I tried that visualization technique and imagined Donna doing Angus Young's duck walk.

But then I remembered I needed to check the oil in the car so that created a whole new image!!!

Anyway, to get back on track.

How and why, I have managed to remain in this job without being arrested, sacked, or sectioned or more likely, a combination of all three, is a tribute to all of them and the many colleagues before them, as well as being somewhat of a mystery to myself and for that there is only one thing to say.

A really big Thank you to you all.

So, finally, it does seem quite obvious that I really lucked out getting that phone call on that Friday afternoon way back in August of 1989 which was for an offer of the job in Dumbarton Academy.

From Arthur, Bob and Peter to Anne, Brian and Dan, I've had many amazing experiences and loads of laughs too. In many ways it has been the centre of my universe for a long, long time but as I said, it could literally have been for anywhere in Strathclyde. Anywhere at all.

And worse still, it could have been in my other subject that I was technically qualified to teach.

I could have been a *Physics* teacher!